Longman Structu
Stage 6

Strike The Father Dead

John Wain
Abridged and simplified by S. H. Burton

Longman

Longman Group UK Limited
Longman House, Burnt Mill, Harlow,
Essex CM20 2JE, England
and Associated Companies throughout the world.

This edition © Longman Group Ltd 1978

All rights reserved; no part of this publication may be
reproduced, stored in a retrieval system, or transmitted
in any form or by any means, electronic, mechanical,
photocopying, recording, or otherwise, without
the prior written permission of the Publishers.

This edition first published 1978
Tenth impression 1990

Acknowledgements
The publishers are grateful to Macmillan
London Ltd for permission to publish this
simplified edition.

Produced by Longman Group (FE) Ltd
Printed in Hong Kong

ISBN 0-582-53793-2

Contents

	page
Introduction	v
Chapter 1 Jeremy Coleman runs away	1
Chapter 2 Jeremy in London	5
Chapter 3 Percy Brett	15
Chapter 4 Eleanor and Alfred	25
Chapter 5 Jeremy returns	29
Chapter 6 Professor Coleman meets his son	33
Chapter 7 Sister and brother	39
Chapter 8 Jeremy and Percy in Paris	42
Chapter 9 Goodbye Tim	61
Chapter 10 Jeremy finds himself at last	69
Chapter 11 Father and son	77
Exercises	85

Introduction

John Wain was born in 1925 in Stoke-on-Trent, a city in Staffordshire, in the North Midlands of England. When he left school he went to St John's College, Oxford, where he won a reputation for his learning and criticism. Later, he taught English Literature at Oxford and Reading Universities. In 1955 he retired from his university employment and became a full-time writer.

He has written several novels apart from *Strike The Father Dead*. His first one was called *Hurry on Down*. It was published in 1953 and at once made him widely-known. It was about a subject that English writers and readers found very interesting in the nineteen-fifties: the attitude of clever young people to education. Many university students were not able to accept that their education was giving them a valuable experience. *Hurry on Down* explored this problem and was very popular. *The Contenders* (published 1958) told the story of three young men from Wain's home town. They were rivals at school and in later life. Victory went to the one who found his true work and happiness in his familiar surroundings. The worldly prizes for which the others fought did not bring them real satisfaction. John Wain's characters are often searching for the satisfaction that arises from worthwhile work well done. In *Living in the Present*, his second novel, and *The Young Visitors* (published 1965), he explored social subjects and criticized the civilization of post-war Britain.

Wain has also written short stories (for example, *Nuncle and Other Stories*) and he is well-known as a poet. He has taught in the United States and in the Soviet Union and he has often given talks on the British radio, as well as writing about films and books in newspapers. Many good judges consider that his criticism of literature (for example, *Preliminary Essays*) is some of the best work of this kind that has been written since the war. His recent book, *Samuel Johnson* (published 1974), delighted the admirers of that great Englishman and increased the reputation of his fellow-countryman, John Wain.

The title of *Strike The Father Dead* was taken from Shakespeare's play *Troilus and Cressida*. In a great speech in that play, Ulysses describes the evils that fall upon a country when *degree* is not obeyed. (We can translate *degree* as meaning order, respect, or a sense of duty.) Disorder is victorious and civilization breaks up. The misery of the situation is described in these words:
Strength shall be lord of imbecility
And the rude [*violent* or *savage*] son shall strike the father dead.

Of course, as John Wain's novel makes plain, the rulers and the older people have a duty to earn and to deserve respect. They cannot expect to be obeyed just because they are older. They must discuss and explain. They must listen to and try to understand the young people to whom they are giving orders. In the end, their position depends on understanding and love. Jeremy tries to revenge himself upon his father. He wants to cut his father out of his life – to 'strike the father dead.' Professor Coleman is greatly to blame for this unhappy situation, for he has made no real effort to understand his son. His sister Eleanor finds it very hard to understand Jeremy's ideas, but she trusts in the power of love and she is never as wrong about Jeremy as her brother is. The father and the son have been separated for many years before they learn to trust each other.

The art of jazz music plays an important part in this book. Jeremy's ambition to became a jazz pianist seems a complete waste of time to his father. Professor Coleman does not understand jazz and he regards this form of music with disgust. It is outside his experience and he believes that Jeremy's love of jazz will destroy him. He cannot accept that jazz demands hard work, self-discipline and imagination. For Jeremy, jazz is all-important. He knows that he has a natural skill and he is determined to develop this skill until he becomes a true artist. Jazz also represents freedom. It provides Jeremy with an escape from the prison in which his father tries to enclose him.

Two men whom Jeremy meets after he has run away from home help him to grow up. Their influence upon him forms his character. First, there is Tim, the cheerful fellow whom he meets at the jazz club. For a long time, Jeremy admires his gay and carefree attitude to life. He compares him with his father, who is always talking about duty. Tim, a good companion, never talks about duty. He lives in the present and enjoys his life. Gradually, Jeremy discovers that Tim cannot be trusted. Tim pursues his own pleasure at the expense of other people and damages those whom he ought to protect. He has no sense of responsibility; and his heartless behaviour to his wife and children forces Jeremy to examine his own way of life.

Percy Brett, the black jazz musician, is the other great influence on Jeremy. Although Jeremy does not realize it, Percy takes the place of the father that Jeremy has lost. Jeremy admires him as an artist, for he recognizes in Percy the excellence that he hopes to reach in time. Playing jazz with Percy teaches Jeremy how to be an artist. Percy's example provides him with the vision that he needs.

But Percy's influence goes beyond jazz. Big and strong though he is, he is gentle. He is a man of peace, full of sympathy and understanding. He is older than Jeremy and knows much more about life, but he treats Jeremy seriously and listens to him with attention. Percy is a man to depend on. Their friendship is built on trust.

Most important, Percy has suffered. As a black man, he has met with insults and injustices, but he has become neither bitter nor violent. He lives his life with cheerful courage, faithful to his art and to his friends. Percy's steady character provides Jeremy with the calm centre that his troubled life lacks.

Strike The Father Dead was recognized as an important book when it was first published and it has held its interest ever since. The character of Jeremy contains the strengths and the weaknesses typical of many young people. Older readers, too, recognize in his development a reflection of their own experiences when they were young. This skilful picture of a very human hero is drawn in loving detail.

Jeremy's story gains added force from the two chief problems with which he has to deal. Old people and young people often misunderstand each other. Then they behave badly. Nowadays, that problem is often referred to as the 'generation gap'. It is the cause of much unhappiness. The other problem is represented through Jeremy's friendship with Percy Brett and the violence with which they are attacked. The race problem creates misery and suffering in many countries today.

It is good to remember that Jeremy and his father reach an understanding in the end; and that they stand side by side with Percy to fight against racial injustice.

Chapter 1
Jeremy Coleman runs away

I remember the moment when I decided to be free. I was just seventeen. I had returned to school after a miserable holiday at home and my father was expecting me to work hard for the summer examination.

I must explain that my father – Professor Alfred Coleman – was a teacher at a university. He was determined that I should be a success at school and become a university teacher too. He was certain that he knew what was best for me. He knew what was best for everybody. Believing in duty and hard work, he was a severe judge of those who did not share his opinions.

My ideas about life were different from his, but I could not explain my hopes and ambitions to him. He did not think that a boy of seventeen could possibly take sensible decisions. My life had to follow the pattern that he had made for me. We could not talk together because we did not understand each other.

I could not discuss my love of music with him – especially the sort of music that I most loved to play. Professor Alfred Coleman thought that jazz was just a horrible noise. He never listened to it. He knew nothing about it, but he had decided that it was not 'proper' music. It was not *art*. If he heard me playing jazz on the piano in the music room at home he was displeased. He would open the door and ask, 'Are you quite sure you've got time for that?' And as he said the word *that* he nodded his head towards the piano. Usually, I played jazz only when I was sure that he was out. According to him I was wasting my time when I wasn't studying my school books. He didn't realize that I had the skill to become a really good jazz musician. I daren't tell him that that was what I wanted to be. He neither knew

1

nor cared. It often seemed to me that the sixty-four black and white keys of the piano were my only friends in the world.

That wasn't true, of course. Aunt Eleanor loved me and did her best for me. She was my father's sister – younger than he was. My mother died when I was a little boy and Aunt Eleanor came to look after us. She wasn't severe like my father but she'd grown up in his shadow. Her clever brother Alfred was always right. She had a great respect for his opinions and she was afraid of arguing with him. In any case, she knew no more about jazz than he did. If Alfred said it was a waste of time, then it *was* a waste of time. She couldn't understand the beauty of its sound: full of colour, life, depth. She couldn't realize what jazz meant to me: it was opposite in every way to the university life that my father was trying to push me into.

So, poor Aunt Eleanor's love wasn't much help to me; and I was beginning to think that my father was my enemy.

It was early summer, and I had a free hour or two one afternoon. I was out on my bicycle, pedalling away from school. I wanted an afternoon off. It was a magical day. The sky was a soft, pale blue; the sun was warm; a gentle wind blew just as it liked. It was wonderful. I pedalled a long way and I began to feel hot and thirsty. I stopped at a cottage and asked for a glass of water. I still remember how good it tasted. Then I got on my bike again and set off, but I had no more heart for pedalling. I wanted to lie down in the grass and have a good long rest. The trouble was that the grass was wet and uncomfortable to lie down in. Then I saw a barn in a field, so I hid my bike in a hedge and walked across to the barn.

It was empty except for some sacks that had once contained cattle food. I climbed up on to the pile of sacks and found a hollow place on the other side. It made a very comfortable bed. The barn was warm and quiet and I floated away into a delightful dreamy state of mind. Soon, I was deep asleep.

How long I slept I don't know. I woke to the sound of a girl's voice: 'Where are you from?'

She was a pretty little thing, dressed in the uniform of the Women's Land Army. She was about my age and she looked very attractive in those clothes. I stood up, thinking what hard work it was for these Land Army girls. It was wartime then. Girls were doing men's work on the farms while the men were away fighting.

'Where are you from?'

I named the school.

'Oh. I thought I hadn't seen you round here.'

'We don't get out much,' I said. My answer made school seem like prison.

'You've cycled a long way, haven't you? What time do you have to get back?'

'It doesn't matter,' I said. I could not let her think I was worried about school rules.

'I was at school myself until I came here. I hated it so much that I joined the Land Army as soon as I could.'

She led the way out of the barn and towards the farmhouse. As we walked together she told me that her name was Nancy. She worked for Mr Upjohn. He, his wife, their son and Nancy did all the work on this big farm. 'We could do with some help,' she said. 'Why don't you work here?'

When we reached the farmhouse Nancy said, 'We're just going to have tea. You've come a long way and you must have something to eat.'

She introduced me to Mrs Upjohn and I sat down at the kitchen table. The farmer's wife put more food on my plate for tea than I would have got at school in a whole day.

I was enjoying myself. The food was wonderful, Nancy was pretty, and school seemed very far away. I was going to be in trouble when I got back but I didn't let that worry me.

When I'd finished eating, Nancy got up to help Mrs Upjohn with the dishes. As they folded the tablecloth I heard her say, 'Jeremy is looking for a job.' She certainly didn't waste time.

'Is he?' replied the farmer's wife. 'We've been talking about some extra help. Mr Upjohn will have to decide when he returns from market. He won't be long.'

'I'll wait outside,' I answered. I walked off towards where I had hidden my bike. It was time to be going. Nancy was getting me into a lot of trouble.

She followed me. 'Where are you going?' she asked.

'I'm going to get my bike,' I said. 'I'm going back –' I was going to say 'Back to school', but suddenly my throat closed over the words. A new life was opening for me. How could I think of going back to school? I was tired of school rules. I was tired of being a boy. I was ready to be a man. I *had* to escape.

'All right,' I said. 'I'll wait for Mr Upjohn.'

'That's good,' she said.

Waiting was horrible. All my doubts and fears returned. They would have missed me at school by now. Had they telephoned home? I tried not to think about that. I kept on imagining Aunt Eleanor's face. If only she won't cry, I thought. I'd always hated doing anything to hurt Aunt Eleanor. Of course, she had often been hurt. Placed as she was between my father and me, she couldn't avoid being hurt. But she always did her best for both of us and I was near to tears when I thought about her. 'God,' I remember thinking, 'if only it were possible to live without hurting anybody.' But even then I knew it wasn't.

Mr Upjohn came back at about nine o'clock. He was a big, good-looking man and he spoke to me kindly.

'Have you left school?'

'Yes,' I answered. It was true, too, I thought. I'd been there this morning and this afternoon I left.

'What attracts you to farm work?'

'I want a job before I go into the Army. I'm not old enough yet to be a soldier.'

There was a long pause. Then he smiled at me. 'It won't do, my boy,' he said. 'You've run away from school, haven't you?'

Mrs Upjohn turned to her husband and said, 'It doesn't matter, Tom. He's only been away from school for a few hours. He can go back tomorrow morning.'

'That's right,' he said. 'You must go back to school tomorrow. I don't know what story you'll tell them when you get back.'

They made me very welcome and I slept in their spare bedroom. I dreamt about Nancy, but when I went downstairs the next morning I did not see her. She was working in the fields with the farmer and his son. Mrs Upjohn gave me a big breakfast. She told me that I was a good boy, but a bit wild. She said I must go back to school and work hard and not cause my family any more worry. I thanked her and said goodbye. Then I found my bike where I'd hidden it and I pedalled off. Not towards school, of course. I was not the same person as I had been before coming to the farm. I'd tasted freedom. I'd changed too much to return to schoolbooks and lessons. I couldn't go back to the things my father thought were good for me.

I rode to the nearest town and sold my bike to a dealer. Then I went to the railway station and bought a ticket to London.

Chapter 2
Jeremy in London

For two reasons, London was the obvious place to make for. First, I could get lost there. If my father asked the police to search for me they wouldn't find me easily in that enormous city. The worst of the bombing – the terrible

London 'blitz' – was over. For two or three years, until the rocket attack at the end of the war, there were hardly any bombs. London was the place where men on leave from the forces enjoyed themselves. It was full of soldiers, sailors and airmen looking for entertainment before they went back to duty. There wasn't anything you couldn't buy. Everybody was looking for some fun – and they wanted it *now*, this minute. These conditions were very convenient for the large number of citizens who were anxious to hide themselves. They had decided to disappear quietly and, for their own various reasons, they wanted to avoid the attention of the officials. Criminals, men who had escaped national service, people who were tired of their earlier lives – it made no difference. There was a place for everybody in wartime London, and no questions were asked.

I hadn't run away from the Army, of course, because I hadn't joined. I was too young for military service when I cleared off from school. I suppose that if I *had* stayed on at school I'd have joined the Army when I was old enough. No doubt I'd have put up with it like most people of my age. But finding myself outside that net I didn't have a bad conscience about staying outside it. For seventeen years my father had been talking to me about duty and self-sacrifice and I was tired of those ideas. He had been a soldier in World War I. He hadn't waited to be ordered to join the Army but had offered himself for military service in 1914. I didn't see why I should do the same. It was a different war and I was a different person from my father. No: no Army for me, thanks! Here was London, a big city into which I could disappear. I disappeared.

The second reason for going to London was that I could get a job there. I could get work as a pianist – the only work that interested me. Jazz was the one thing I lived for. To sit down at a piano, run my fingers along the keys, and think of all the lovely jazz that was waiting to burst out of the piano! I often feel like that still. At seventeen, I felt like

it all the time. And there was jazz in London then. Before 1939 very few English people wanted to hear jazz. When the USA entered the war in 1941, American soldiers came to England. Many of them were fond of jazz and many English people learned to enjoy it too. By 1942 there was an audience for jazz. American soldiers spent a lot of their free time and their money in night clubs and restaurants where jazz was played.

It took me about three days to find a job playing the piano in a little club near King's Cross. It wasn't a very good club and it wasn't a very good job. The owner paid me just enough to live on but I didn't mind the poor wages. I had a piano to play and people to listen to my music. The club made its money by selling drinks and sandwiches and charging a lot for them. I gradually realized that some of the customers came because they liked my playing. God bless them! I don't remember their names or their faces, but they were my first regular audience. They were my fans. I played that piano for them with all my heart. My ten fingers made it sing jazz to them. My fans listened. It was a new world, a great morning. I don't believe that the early jazzmen such as Jelly Roll Morton ever felt prouder than I did then. I was 'Mr Jazz'. Nobody was ever more determined than I. All I did was play the piano. I had forgotten home, family, the war, time, nature and death. The whole of my world was contained in the sixty-four black and white keys of the piano and the smoky little club in which I played it every night. So, naturally, my playing got better day by day. By the time Christmas 1943 came, I was really playing jazz.

Among the regular customers of the club was a man called Tim. He was a fast-talking little chap, full of jokes. He could make a success of any party. You couldn't be serious when Tim was around. I came to know him very soon; he was the first club member to speak to me.

I'd been playing one night, from about nine o'clock to

twelve, without a rest. At midnight I left the piano and went down the room to get a drink at the bar. I had some beer, I remember. I'd just begun to like the taste of the drink. It was cool and refreshing as it slipped down my throat.

I swallowed one quickly and put my empty glass down on the bar. As I turned round I found this chap Tim standing beside me.

'Have a drink on me,' he said. 'That was great piano-playing tonight.'

'You think so?' I said, trying not to seem too eager for praise.

'You were great,' he repeated. 'I've heard most of the best jazzmen and your playing compares very well with theirs.'

At once I began questioning him eagerly about which of the great piano players he had heard. I didn't get much information out of him. He didn't seem certain whether he had heard them alive or on a record player. His memory of their names seemed confused. But I didn't suspect him and we chatted on. Before I noticed, we'd had quite a lot to drink. I was drinking beer, he was on whisky.

'You know, you make a lot of difference to this club,' he said, smiling at me. 'It used to be only Maureen who made the place worth coming to. Now there's you as well.'

Maureen was the girl who sold drinks at the bar. I had never thought that she was particularly attractive. I soon learned that Tim could not resist anything in a skirt. He went on with his chat, aiming it half at Maureen and half at me, and swallowing two more whiskies as he talked. It was amusing and lighthearted, and I enjoyed it.

At last, I went back to the piano, feeling glad that I had made a friend. I played for about an hour before taking another rest. When I returned to the bar Tim had gone, but Maureen was waiting for me. She told me that there were three glasses of beer and five whiskies to pay for. I said that there must have been a mistake. Tim had asked me to have a drink on him. Surely he should pay for at least one of the beers and some of the whisky?

'Well, he didn't pay,' Maureen said. 'Don't make me stand here arguing.'

So I paid. I didn't mind. Tim was an amusing companion even if he was short of money. I was employed at the club and could buy the drinks cheaper than he could.

A day or two later I saw him again. I was walking past a public house near my lodgings, when I heard someone knocking on the window of the pub. There was Tim inviting me inside.

'Well, this is luck,' he said as I entered. 'I was just ready for a drink with a friend.'

He began to chat in his own entertaining way. While he talked, the pub was filling up. Tim seemed to know everyone who came in. Soon, everybody was listening to one of his stories and laughing. One of the men had asked him why he wasn't in the forces. Tim replied with a very funny account of his medical examination for the Royal Air Force. Nobody believed him, but it was so comical that we all laughed. According to Tim's story, the doctors discovered during his medical examination that he was a very sick man. He acted the whole thing in front of us. Doctor after doctor came into the medical room and each discovered a new disease in Tim. Not a word of it was true, but we all enjoyed it. It was a wonderfully comical performance.

At the end of the performance I asked Tim to have a drink on me. He refused and bought me one instead. In fact, he bought me several, and a sandwich as well. I thought that he might try to borrow the money off me. I liked Tim and I was beginning to admire him. Yet I couldn't believe that he really meant to buy me a drink. I was seeing him in daylight for the first time and he didn't look like a man with spare money. In the artificial lighting of the club he didn't look poor. When he was there, his short, fattish figure and fashionable moustache suggested that he was a man who had plenty of money. But in the clear light of day I could see how shabby he was. His clothes were dirty and worn-out. His shoes were cracked. He didn't seem to worry about being shabby. It was hard to imagine Tim worrying about anything.

I watched him as he chatted to me. I tried to find out what he was really like. I might as well have tried to catch a smoke-ring. I had never met anybody who seemed to enjoy life so much. Life was exciting to him. Tim was a new experience for me; especially as, to me, he was quite old. (He was about twenty-five, but you must remember that I wasn't quite eighteen at the time.) That a man should have reached his age and remained gay – that he should care so little about his shabby clothes! But I had only my father and my schoolteachers to compare him with. Oh yes, I decided that I admired Tim and that I wanted to be like him. But he was just as much a mystery as ever.

We left the pub together and I went back to my lodgings. But I went on thinking about Tim. I hadn't, after all, had to spend my own money. He really had bought me those drinks. So he had got some money somehow, though he didn't seem to have a job.

After that, I spent more and more time with Tim. We became good friends. But our real friendship began on that wonderful evening at the club when Tim introduced me to Percy – and Percy introduced me to jazz.

Chapter 3
Percy Brett

This is how I first met Percy. Three Royal Air Force men had come to the club. They loved jazz and they had often come before to hear me play. They had told me that they played jazz in their spare time at their Air Force Camp.

One played drums, one played the saxophone, and one the double bass. I'd suggested that they should bring their instruments to the club. They needed a piano player to make up a proper jazz group.

Their Air Force Camp was quite near to London but I was surprised when they walked in, carrying their musical instruments. During the war, plans were often made but not carried out. Those men could have been moved to Africa or Greenland, or anywhere, before the weekend. But there they were, in the club, and we were playing jazz together.

I didn't know how good they would be. The invitation was a risk. But they *were* good. It was the first time that I had played jazz in a group. I had always played the piano on my own. Now, suddenly, I had the drums and the double bass to support me with rhythm and the saxophone to supply a line of melody. Between and against the rhythm of the drums and the double bass and the melody of the saxophone my piano found a new freedom. Now, for the first time, I discovered the full voice of jazz. It was like growing a new set of limbs. I felt light, as if I could walk up and down walls and jump over houses.

It happened to be my birthday – and it was heaven. Wine flowed out from the keys under my fingers. Rhythm came from the drums and double bass, melody from the saxophone, and – in between – my piano was singing jazz. Nothing could possibly go wrong. We were all riding on a joyous wave that would take us wherever we wanted to go. The sound we were making together was the happiest, the most healing, thing in all the world.

We played on for at least two hours before anybody suggested stopping for a drink of beer. When at last we did stop, and went over to the bar, we only wanted to talk about our playing. Then we thought up new ideas to try out. Nobody else existed. Tim was there, whispering across the bar to Maureen, but I was too busy to talk to him.

After a drink or two we hurried away from the bar to start playing again. As I passed Tim he stopped me.

'I've got a great jazz musician here,' he said. 'I brought him along especially.'

I didn't know whether to believe him. How would Tim know a great jazz musician? I didn't want our music-making to be spoilt by Tim or anybody else.

'He's been listening to you all evening,' Tim said. 'Here he is.' He pointed to a big black man who was sitting at a table near the bar.

The lighting in the room wasn't much good but I knew at a glance that I had never seen anyone like him before. He was about my height, but enormously broad. He made me feel like an insect.

'Hey, Percy,' Tim called out, 'come on over and meet Jeremy.'

The black man held out his hand. 'I'm Percy Brett,' he said. He had a wonderfully deep, musical voice.

We shook hands. He bore himself like a nobleman or a king. I felt as if I had been introduced to a royal person. But he was completely natural.

'Percy plays the trumpet,' said Tim, smiling as proudly as if he had taught him.

'Valve trombone, in fact,' said Percy. He corrected Tim gently, as if he were a child who had made an understandable mistake. 'But I play it like a bass trumpet.'

I felt excitement rising in me. These were new ideas in England then, though we are used to them now. Until that night I had never seen a valve trombone.

'Where is it?' I asked. He pointed to a case under his chair.

'Why don't you join us?' I could see that he was eager to play. Although I was young, I had a jazzman's heart and knew when a jazzman felt like playing. 'If we are good enough for you,' I added.

Percy looked at me; then he looked at the Air Force men.

They were waiting, with their instruments ready. Then he nodded several times. 'Yes,' he said. '*Good* enough, yes.' His face split into an enormous smile and his rich laughter rang through the club.

I can still remember the very first notes he blew. The sounds that he produced from that valve trombone were sharp and cutting. He played with immense energy, but he was exact. The jazz that Percy played was new to us. As we played with him we were learning. We were learning with our ears, our hands and our muscles. We knew that this was real, driving jazz. It was as far above what we had been playing as that was above what I had been doing on my own.

A lot of things happened at once. Percy's sudden, swinging horn notes brought the club members to their feet with excitement. At least half of them stood near the band, listening and shouting encouragement. They had never heard a horn played like this before. They had never heard jazz sound like this before. And, at the centre of it all, I felt as if I was playing the whole band with my ten fingers. A jazz pianist always feels like that when things are going well. I was playing the double bass; I was beating the drums; I was blowing Percy's horn. The music was all coming through my brain. Without me, the music would stop and the musicians themselves would disappear.

Suddenly, a crashing noise interrupted us. Our music died in mid-air. I looked down the room. A table was lying on its side. That must have been the noise that stopped us. Standing round it, shouting, were half-a-dozen men. Tim was one of them. I rushed to see if I could help him. Before I reached them, Tim's voice had silenced the others. He shouted his words at a big man with red hair.

'Uniform! What do you think I was wearing when I was wounded? I was a soldier before you put on a uniform!'

The owner of the club pushed through the crowd. He put his hand on Tim's arm. 'Now, Tim, now, Tim,' he said.

Tim pushed him away. 'No, I'll finish now I've begun. I was fighting for my country before this man joined the Army. How dare he ask me why I am not in uniform?'

By this time the red-haired man was beaten. He went and found his coat and left quietly. Everybody was in sympathy with Tim.

We returned to our places and began to play again. Somehow, I couldn't stop thinking about Tim and the strange world in which he lived. He seemed to believe the lies that he told. Or perhaps he did not believe anything? These doubts affected my music. I was not playing nearly as well as I had been doing.

We carried on until the last members left the club and then, between two and three o'clock in the morning, we sat down to eat a very late supper – or was it a very early breakfast? All of us who had been playing jazz together were there. Tim sat down with us as naturally as if his scene with the red-haired man had qualified him to join the club staff of entertainers.

Percy Brett was the centre of attention. He was by far the best jazz musician at that table. He was also the strongest character. We all felt that we were small compared with Percy. His big head, big body and black face made him different. It was more than that, though that would have been enough. His character was big. He had done things, seen things, *been* things, outside our experience. He sat there like a king. But he smiled and was friendly to us all.

He had to be back at his American Air Force camp at eight o'clock that morning. I went to the railway station with him. I didn't want to part from him. We were talking about jazz all the time.

'I'll be lucky to get the chance to play with another real jazzman,' I said.

Percy looked at me. 'You liked tonight?' he asked. 'You learned something?'

'You know I did.'

'Well', he said, 'we can have five more Saturday nights like this. I'll be at this Air Force Camp for another five weeks. After that, we move. I can play at your club for five more Saturday nights – if you want me to.'

For the next five weeks, Percy and Tim were at the centre of my life. A boy of eighteen is influenced by older people. He is either going to copy them or fight against them. I'd been fighting against my father all my life. I didn't fight against Percy or Tim. They gave me ideas that I'd never had before. Percy taught me about jazz. Both he and Tim taught me about life. But they were very different men and their lessons were different. I learned gradually that Percy had been roughly treated when he was young. Like most black people in America then, he had been poor. His education had been neglected. But he did not ask for pity and he did not waste time in complaining. He had his music and he was proud of his skill and of the independence it had brought him. Although he owed little to the USA, he did not grumble about being in the Air Force. Percy's ideas about duty and honour were just as strong as my father's. Different, of course – and *he* didn't keep on talking about them.

Tim had other ideas. He pleased himself. The only rules that he obeyed were his own rules. Tim didn't worry about other people. He did what he wanted to do. After seventeen years of listening to my old man's lessons, I found Tim's attitude to life very attractive.

The weeks passed. One Saturday, Percy told us that he was going to be moved. He didn't know where he was going.

'Meet me next Thursday,' said Tim. 'I'll arrange a surprise for you both.' He went away to make his arrangements.

'What a man!' I said.

Percy smiled. 'It's a pity he doesn't play jazz,' he said. 'We could use him.'

We sat in silence for a few moments. 'Where do you think you might be going, Percy?' I asked.

He shook his head. 'They don't tell you. You get your orders and you go.'

'That's terrible,' I said. 'You aren't being treated like a human being.'

'I have never been treated like a human being,' said Percy.

I didn't really know what he was talking about.

'You mean...' I began.

'I'm black,' said Percy. 'Black men aren't treated like human beings.'

'They are in England,' I said.

'Are they?'

Percy didn't discuss it any more. He knew how little knowledge I had.

Thursday arrived and Tim met Percy and me. He was driving a big car and he had plenty of petrol. We asked him whose it was but he only laughed.

'You've been good boys,' he said, 'and your Uncle Tim's going to take you for a drive.'

We drove away and I suddenly realized that we really were going for a drive in the country. The country! I'd forgotten it existed. For months I'd seen nothing but streets, and even those I'd hardly seen in daylight. It hadn't mattered to me, because all the colour and freshness I needed had been coming to me from music. Now, it was wonderful to be going into the fields. The weather was perfect. It was one of those unusual days in early December when the sun is shining with the last warmth of the year. We drove out of bombed, dark, dirty London towards the sunny, smiling country.

The memory of that day lasted for years. We were all three happy and contented. We stopped at several old country pubs and drank good beer. We had lunch at a hotel in a market town. I felt so peaceful and so full of love for everyone that I bought a picture-postcard at a village post office and sent it to Aunt Eleanor. I told her that I was all right and that I was earning my living as a pianist in a club. I didn't give her my address, but I thought the postcard would stop her worrying. I didn't like to think of how much I had upset Aunt Eleanor.

Night fell and we turned towards the city. It started to rain as Tim drove through streets that I did not recognize. He parked the car in a big garage and got out. 'Come on,' he said.

'Where are we going?'

'Just part of Uncle Tim's present for two good boys,' he said. 'Follow me and don't ask awkward questions.'

He led the way into a big building divided into flats. We climbed the stairs and Tim produced a bunch of keys, showing us into a very comfortable room. Soon, we were sitting round a big electric fire and drinking good wine out of very expensive glasses.

'Whose flat is this?' I asked him.

'Ours, for as long as we want it.'

'Look at all that music!' Percy exclaimed. He was standing by the record player and drawing record after record out of the cupboard. Mozart, Beethoven, Brahms, Schumann... all the great composers were there. And Percy wanted to hear them all. He was really annoyed that he couldn't listen to six or seven records at the same time.

'Do you hear that? Do you hear that?' he kept saying to me.

'Of course I hear it,' I'd say.

'No, but *that*,' he'd answer, pointing with his finger as if he could actually *show* me the sound written in the air above the record player.

Tim brought food in from the kitchen and we stopped the music while we ate.

'That's one thing I'll have when the war is over and I get

out of the Force,' said Percy. 'Records, records, records and more records. I never had the chance to listen much. Too many people living in our house when I was a boy – and no records like those.'

'But do you mean to say that you haven't heard the great composers before?'

He smiled. 'Oh, I've heard them. I've taken my chances. I've been to a lot of concerts since I joined the US Air Force. They let you in if you're in uniform.'

'Let you in...?' I asked. I realized again how little I knew about Percy's life.

'Yes,' said Percy. 'Where I lived when I was young, they didn't let you in to concerts if you were black. Big concerts were for white people. I used to stand outside the concert hall and listen. I was learning music then from a black teacher and I used to write the notes down when I heard things that stuck in my memory. A lot of the music did and I heard some of it again tonight. That's why I was so excited. It was music that I'd copied in my notebook and played on my horn.'

I wanted him to go on talking. I was learning about his life. But the door opened and a woman walked in. She was about ten years older than Tim and she looked at him as if she hated him. I didn't need telling who she was. It was obvious that she owned the flat. She gave Percy and me one cold glance, then turned back to Tim.

He moved towards her, trying to smile. 'Helen!' he said, 'I thought you were away this weekend.'

'I know you did.' She sounded as if she could murder him. 'I came back to tell you something. I came to tell you to get out. I want you out of this flat immediately.'

'It's rather sudden, isn't it?' asked Tim. He spoke as if it didn't matter to him. I had to admire his spirit but I didn't want to watch the scene.

'For two years,' Helen said, 'you've been comfortable, living here, using my money, and cheating me. Well, now

23

it's finished, as you always knew it would be sooner or later. I've had enough of you. I wish I could hurt you. I wish I could make you ashamed of yourself.'

'Well, you can't, so forget it,' Tim answered.

By this time Percy and I were out of the door. We went down the stairs into the cold night and Percy made his first and last remark about the affair.

'It looks as if Tim had better get some cards printed.'

'Cards?'

'Change of address cards,' said Percy; and his deep laughter rang through the empty street. He started to walk without any hesitation, as if Tim and the car and our day's holiday had all died a natural death and buried themselves. I walked by his side, content to be with him, and not asking where we were going. But we hadn't walked far before we heard Tim's light, amused voice behind us.

'Wait!' he called. 'Wait for me, you chaps.'

We waited and he caught us up. He had some sort of rough bundle under his arm. 'Well,' he said, 'that's the end of my life as a writer.'

'Your what?' asked Percy, looking at him solemnly, but obviously ready to laugh at any moment.

'My life as a writer. Didn't know that I was a great but unrecognized writer? I had a play planned out in my head. It was a great play. In fact, I had several great plays in my mind. All I needed was peace and quiet in which to write them. I got a lot of good ideas while I was living in Helen's flat.'

'You don't mean to tell me,' I said, 'that you've been living free by pretending to be a writer.'

'It was a bit more complicated than that,' said Tim. 'But I see we're approaching a pub. Inside, chaps, and I'll tell you all about it while we swallow some drinks.'

Percy, as usual, paid. Tim emptied his first glass very quickly. He began to talk confidently. 'You see, Helen was part of the "S.T.P". The Save Tim Plan. Everyone connected with it works to save Tim from the unpleasant things of life – work and hunger and worry.'

I suddenly realized that Percy and I were in the Save Tim Plan – without knowing it. Well, does it matter? I thought. We get plenty of fun out of Tim in return for what we give him.

'Helen,' he said, 'was the most important member of the "S.T.P." She had a good job and plenty of money. I lived very comfortably with her. But I *did* give her something in return. I amused her. She wasn't lonely. I used to tell her about my ideas for plays. She liked to believe that she was supporting a great writer. It wasn't true, of course, but it made her feel good. Oh, I knew how to deal with Helen – until she couldn't put up with me any longer. I've had two very sheltered years with her – but now, poor old Tim's out in the cold world again.'

'You were lucky,' I said. 'It's a pity it's over now.'

He smiled. 'That's how things happen. Up for a time; down for a time. I don't let life worry *me*.' As he reached for a cigarette out of Percy's packet, the bundle that he had been carrying rolled off his knees. It fell to the floor and before he could gather it up I saw what it contained. A razor, a shaving-brush, a comb, one clean shirt; all his possessions, wrapped in a towel.

But the towel was a thick, expensive one. It must have been Helen's.

Chapter 4
Eleanor and Alfred

When the school telephoned Alfred to say that Jeremy had run away, I was terribly worried. I begged Alfred to try to find him and at first I could not believe that he did not intend to. I couldn't eat or sleep; I lived on cups of tea for almost a week. One morning, at breakfast, Alfred talked very seriously to me. He accused me of allowing myself to enjoy my sorrow.

I put the tea pot down so hard that it made him jump. '*Enjoying* my *sorrow?*' I shouted. (I had hardly ever spoken angrily to him before.) 'Wouldn't it be more true to say that you were enjoying your calmness and self-control? Jeremy, your only son, has disappeared and you sit there eating your breakfast and accusing me of enjoying my unhappiness!'

He held up his hand for silence. It was one of his habits that most annoyed me, but I had to listen to him. He spoke gently: 'You have always been kind and loving to Jeremy, my dear, but you must learn to bear the truth. The facts are ugly. We know that he is not in hospital, so he has not had an accident. Nor has he been arrested by the police. Jeremy has *chosen* to disappear.'

'You know very well,' I answered, 'that Jeremy is as stubborn as you are. He won't come home if he has to be humble and admit that he is wrong. You must find him and *ask* him to come home.'

As I spoke I saw Alfred's face set in that stubborn expression of his. He hates to be reminded that Jeremy is like him. 'You must know,' I went on, 'how Jeremy must be feeling, because you are the same yourself. You'd – '

Alfred interrupted me. 'I don't wish to hear you repeating that Jeremy's character is like mine. I have had to train myself to become as I am. I have learned self-discipline. I have taught myself to do my duty. I believe in service to others. Do you call that stubborn?'

'And you expect Jeremy to do the same? Why, he's only – '

'You need not remind me that my son is young. I know his exact age. I do not expect young people to be as disciplined as older ones. Jeremy, I am sure, could train his character most successfully – if he *wanted* to.'

There was a silence. I didn't want to argue with him about Jeremy's character. I knew that Jeremy had done wrong in running away from school. But I didn't see how that affected our attitude. Surely we should be trying to get him back?

'I understand how you feel, Alfred, but we are still responsible for Jeremy. We still love him. We ought to be trying to find him. Once we knew where he was we could at least offer him our love and understanding.'

His face was stiff and hard again. 'The school has made all the usual enquiries,' he said. 'The headmaster feels responsible for keeping in touch with the police. It is not good for a school's reputation when a boy runs away.'

'And what about his home?' I asked. There were tears in my eyes. 'What sort of a home is it? He doesn't come to us; and he doesn't even let us know where he is.' I couldn't talk any more. It was too much for me – the worry, the sleepless nights, and no proper food. I knew that if we didn't get some news of Jeremy soon, I would be ill. But I daren't say so to Alfred. He would have said that I was threatening him.

He sat still, waiting for me to stop crying. He was like a judge at a trial. I made several attempts to speak, then I went out quietly into the garden. I tried to be calm, but I felt so tired and ill. I didn't know what I was going to do.

And I was ill for many weeks. Dr Robinson was puzzled about the cause of my illness. Alfred frequently demanded an explanation, but the doctor could only say that I was 'very disturbed'. That, Alfred replied, was not an explanation at all. Being disturbed, he said, was not a disease. I knew that he was very worried about me. I began to suspect that he was worried about Jeremy, too. He did not talk about it, of course. Alfred's ideas of duty and self-discipline prevented him from discussing his own feelings.

I had terrible dreams in my fever. They were always about Jeremy. He was in great danger and I could not save him. In one horrible dream he was being sacrificed. A priest was reading prayers while men prepared a fire in which Jeremy was to be burnt to death. The priest turned his face to me and I saw that it was Alfred. I screamed, 'Stop those terrible prayers. You are his father, Alfred – his father!'

And I woke up to find Alfred by my bedside. 'Are you calmer now, my dear?' he asked. His eyes were loving and kind, but I turned away. I'd realized that Alfred would not change his mind. He would *not* attempt to find his son.

Once I'd accepted the truth of that I began to get better. 'And besides,' I thought, 'if I die, there'll be nobody in this world who really cares for Jeremy – not as he should be cared for.'

Some weeks later I was in the kitchen making our early morning tea when I heard the postman's knock at the front door. And there, on the mat in the hall, was a picture postcard. A message from Jeremy at last! He said that he was all right. He was making a living with his music. Of course, he didn't say where we could find him, but he had remembered me.

I didn't tell Alfred about the postcard. I was afraid that he might give the information to the police and make trouble for Jeremy. I was determined to reach Jeremy myself. I wanted him to come home. I didn't think he would stay, but at least he could discuss his difficulties with Alfred. But how could I reach him? It was a long time before I solved that problem.

Towards the end of term Alfred invited some of his third-year students to come to our house for a discussion. They arrived after dinner and I took them some tea at about half-past nine. I knew one of them already, a tall young man with red hair and a kind, sensible face. It was easy to arrange that he should help me with the cups and saucers after the meeting.

When he appeared in the kitchen I said, 'Mr Wilbraham, we haven't much time. Will you be in London during the holidays?'

He looked surprised, but answered that he would.

'Then, please, do something for me. It's very important, but you mustn't say anything about it to anyone. Professor Coleman's son, Jeremy, ran away from school months ago. All we know is that he's in London and that he plays the piano at a club.'

'He's a jazz player?'

'Yes – and, please, will you find him and tell him that his Aunt Eleanor is waiting for him to come home. And if he will come home his father will talk to him and everything will be all right.'

I was afraid that Alfred might walk in at any moment and my nervousness prevented me from talking very sensibly. Fortunately, Mr Wilbraham seemed to understand.

'Professor Coleman doesn't know you're looking for him?' he asked.

I shook my head. 'He would be angry if he knew I was trying to reach Jeremy and bring him home. But I do so much want to bring them together, and – ' I couldn't say any more. Tears filled my eyes and I had to turn away.

He put his hand gently on my shoulder. 'Don't worry,' I heard him say. 'I'll find him in the holidays and I'll give him your message. Don't worry – I'll do it.'

I turned round to thank him, but he was gone. I never saw him again, but I often think of him now.

Chapter 5
Jeremy returns

I was playing in the club one evening when a solemn, red-haired, tall chap suddenly appeared at the piano. He said he wanted to speak to me and he had a message from Aunt Eleanor.

'A message from *who*?' I said. I kept on playing softly because I didn't want a nasty silence to attract attention to us. I felt nervous all at once: what was the old thing doing? Had she tracked me down herself? Was this chap about to tell me that she was waiting for me outside?

'From your Aunt Eleanor,' the chap answered. 'Professor Coleman's sister.'

'Yes, I know she's Professor Coleman's sister,' I said, giving him a straight stare. Was he trying to be funny, I wondered? But I could see he wasn't: he was much too serious.

'She says that you must go home and see them,' he said. He obviously wanted to get it over and go. 'She wants you to talk to your father.'

'Did she say anything else?'

'She said that everything would be all right,' the red-haired chap replied. He gave me a last glance, turned away from the piano, and moved towards the door.

'Wait a minute,' I called weakly. I hadn't really got anything to ask him, but his sudden appearing and disappearing seemed all wrong. I knew he must be one of my father's students, but how had Aunt Eleanor managed to put him on my tracks? And then, of course, I remembered the postcard I had sent her. Given that, it hadn't been difficult for him to find me.

The club members were looking enquiringly at me. They wanted to know where the music was. I saw the red-haired chap near the door. 'Thanks for the message from home,' I called. And I turned back to my sixty-four black and white keys – my faithful friends – and I got on with my job.

After that meeting my peace of mind was gone. It was strange how near to me that message seemed to bring Aunt Eleanor and my father. The student so obviously belonged to their world and not to mine. He had been so nervous in the club. He probably thought that it was a wicked place, and he was eager to get away. I could not doubt that Aunt Eleanor and my father would feel the same about a jazz club. My present life would seem useless – perhaps evil – to them.

I began to wonder what was happening to them. Were they very worried about me? (I knew they must be, of course.) What did they think had happened to me? I blamed myself for forgetting them for so long. I had been unkind. They were people – and you can't throw people away like rubbish.

But if I let them interfere with my life they could do me a lot of harm. I was breaking the law by not joining the Army. Supposing that I went to see them, they might telephone the police and report me. I had to laugh at that thought. It was impossible to imagine them doing such a thing as that. The worst result of a visit would be an unhappy, perhaps an angry, conversation with my old man.

And what would be the best result of a visit? I wasn't sure. I suppose that I wanted to build a friendship with the old man. It hurts when you feel that your father is your enemy. I'd lived independently for some time and I hadn't asked him for any help. So perhaps he would respect my independence and recognize that I was right to take my own decisions about my own life.

Funny! The old man didn't give in so easily. But I had some hope and on the next Sunday I got on a train. I wasn't very happy about my visit, but I thought I ought to try to be friends with them. I didn't warn them that I was coming. I thought it was better to surprise them.

The station, the town and the quiet, Sunday-afternoon streets were just as I remembered them. Nothing had changed. Why should it? I hadn't been away for very long. Yet it seemed somehow unnatural that everything should be the same as it had always been. Without letting myself think, I marched along 'our' road just as if I was returning from a Sunday walk. But I knocked on the front door like a visitor.

As I knocked, fear hit me. My mouth went dry and I

prayed that Aunt Eleanor and not the old man would open the door. Or perhaps they were both out. In that case, I could push a note through the letter-box and go back to London without seeing them.

I was getting excited about nothing, of course. The old man never did answer a knock at the door. Besides, on Sunday afternoons he usually went up to his study and got on with his work. When he wasn't on duty at the university he kept himself busy with a big and very important book that he'd been writing for years.

As I was thinking about all this, the door opened, and there stood Aunt Eleanor.

'Hello,' I said, trying to sound quite calm. 'I hope I haven't given you a shock.'

She held on to the door very tightly, but she managed to answer me quietly. 'No,' she said, 'you haven't given me a shock. I've been expecting you since I sent that student to find you and give you my message. Come in.'

She gave me a quick kiss and then took me into the kitchen. 'Your father's upstairs in his study, as usual. I knew you'd arrive without warning us and I made up my mind that I wouldn't say anything to him. It will be a shock for him. He knows nothing about your postcard or about the message I sent you.'

'How did you know that I'd come without warning?' I asked.

'Oh,' she said, 'old aunts understand more than their nephews sometimes realize.'

I stored that remark away to think about in the future. My immediate problem was how to deal with the old man.

'How have you been?' I asked her. I'd suddenly realized how much older she looked and I knew that it was my fault.

'I've been very well, thank you,' she said. 'And so has your father. We've been anxious, of course, but we knew that you would be all right.'

'Aunt Eleanor,' I said. 'Let's have a bargain. Don't treat

me as if I am stupid and I won't treat you like that either. Old aunts understand a lot of things, but runaway nephews aren't completely blind. Don't tell me you've been perfectly well, because I can see that you are a lot thinner. I know that you must have suffered a lot because of me. I'm not trying to make excuses. We might as well be honest with each other. I ran away because it was the only thing I could do. I was being forced into a way of life that was no good for me.'

'What kind of life, Jeremy?' she asked, opening her eyes very wide and really trying to understand. 'You were only a boy at school.'

'School was only a part of the trouble,' I said. 'But must I explain all this twice, once for you and once for my father? Can't we fetch him downstairs and talk about it together? Can't the three of us get it all over?'

'No,' she said calmly. 'Not the three of us. Just the two of you. I think it's between you and your father, Jeremy.'

My heart jumped. She was right. I had to do this, but waiting for it to begin was hell.

'All right,' I said, 'but, please, will you fetch him downstairs now – at once?'

She nodded and went off to fetch him. As she passed my chair, she bent down and gave me a quick, light kiss. I suppose, in a way, I was all she had.

Chapter 6
Professor Coleman meets his son

It began as just another Sunday afternoon. I had a short rest after lunch then went upstairs to my study to get on with some work. No sooner was I really interested in a difficult problem about literature than Eleanor entered the room. She told me that Jeremy had arrived and that he wished to see me. Then she left the study as suddenly as she

33

had come.

At first, I couldn't believe her news; but I gathered up my books and notes and made my desk tidy. I always leave my desk tidy, of course, but on this occasion I was glad of the excuse to gain a little time. I wanted to collect my thoughts before seeing Jeremy. I was angry with Eleanor and I wasn't thinking very clearly. I felt sure that she had arranged his visit in some way. Why could she not have warned me that he might be coming? I should have been given the opportunity to prepare myself for such an important meeting.

Since he was here it was, of course, my duty to see him, so I went downstairs. At first, I thought I would insist on her being present. Then I went into the room alone. He was standing by the window with his back to me. When he heard the door open, he turned round.

'Hello, father,' he said.

'I'm glad to see you at home, my boy,' I answered. 'I didn't know that you were coming, so I'm – I'm rather...' I hesitated for a suitable word.

'I feel like that, too,' he said, smiling at me. I could see that he was trying to be friendly.

'How long can we expect you to stay?' I asked.

'Only a few hours, I'm afraid. I have to get back to work tonight.'

'Work?'

'Yes. Didn't Aunt Eleanor tell you? I play the piano.'

'And where do you play it?'

'At a club in London – near King's Cross.'

'I hope you'll forgive my curiosity,' I said. 'I've had no information about you for a long time.'

'I'm sorry about that,' he said. 'I didn't want to make you anxious, but it seemed best to disappear for a time.'

I invited him to sit down. As he did so, I looked at him carefully. He was wearing a cheap grey suit and his shoes were old, but he looked healthy. His face hadn't changed.

In my eyes he still looked like a schoolboy.

'I don't expect to be told very much,' I said, 'so I won't ask any more questions. I think we had better forget what has happened in the last year. Then we can make some sensible plans for your future.'

'Listen, father,' he said. 'Let me explain what I am hoping to gain from this visit. I want us to learn to understand each other and to be friends. I haven't come here to explain myself, to give you a report on the last year, or to make promises for the future. You brought me up in the way you thought best. It wasn't what I wanted, but we needn't be bitter about that. I'm sorry that I've made you and Aunt Eleanor worry about me. Now that you've seen me, your worries should be over. You can see that I'm alive and well. I'm earning my own living and there's nothing I want from you. I only want us to be friendly.'

He spoke quickly, as if he didn't care very much about my attitude to what he was saying. But, while he spoke, his eyes were fixed on mine and they seemed anxious. For his own sake, I decided to tell the boy quite firmly what to expect from me.

'Jeremy,' I said, 'you hurried over some rather important points in that last speech of yours, my boy. Perhaps you'll pardon me if I give them some attention. You may expect forgiveness, but you did hurt your Aunt Eleanor and me. Our discussion must start from that fact.'

'I don't *want* any discussion!' he exclaimed. 'I only want – '

'You have already said so,' I interrupted. 'You say you are not here to explain your actions. I must tell you that, if you come to my house at all, you *must* explain yourself.'

He was silent for a moment, not looking at me. When he spoke, his voice was gentle. 'If I thought that explaining would help, I'd do it. But if I explained what is going on in my mind, it would only hurt you more.'

'I shall have to take that risk,' I said firmly.

'Why should you? I could explain a lot of things. The fact is that you brought me up in a particular way – and it was no good to me. You demanded that I should accept your ideas. Live for others. Hard work and self-sacrifice. Discipline. Duty. Don't be tempted by pleasure. When I was young, I tried to accept all that. I thought that your ideas about life must be right. Later, I had to turn them down. I don't see life through your eyes now. I *won't* try to live your kind of life. I don't think that it's made you happy. Oh, I know you'll say that happiness doesn't matter, but I think it does. I think that people should make themselves happy first and then spread that happiness around. If you are not happy yourself, how can you make other people happy?'

I began to see how hopeless the situation was. It was my duty to go on trying as long as he would listen – and I tried. 'Jeremy', I said, 'the word "happy" is not one that I use very much.'

'By God, it isn't!' he exclaimed.

'Impoliteness will not help our discussion.'

'I'm sorry. Do go on.'

'To pursue happiness is dangerous. A man who looks for happiness for himself often finds misery. He makes other people miserable, too.'

'That's where we are different. I think the world is a place in which we should enjoy ourselves. Of course, we must care about other people. If we are happy we *do* care. But to be happy is our first duty. We can't do any good in the world if we are unhappy.'

For a moment I looked at my son as if he were a stranger to me. Where had he learned these poisonous ideas? It was, without doubt, my duty to attack his dangerous opinions.

'You find these ideas attractive, Jeremy. Let me point out that there is another test. The way in which a man lives his life measures the value of his principles. Is your conscience clear about your life during this past year? Has your life proved that your opinions are right?'

'I'm not afraid of that test,' he answered. 'I've done no one any harm. I've worked very hard. I've earned my own living. I've made progress in the art that I want to follow.'

'The...*art*?'

'Yes...*art*. Playing the piano. Learning to become a good jazz pianist.'

'Ah! *Jazz*! I must allow others to decide whether jazz can be described as art. You say that you perform this... this *art* in a club near King's Cross. Can you tell me anything about this club?'

'Come and see for yourself.'

'Thank you,' I said. 'I am too old to visit a night-club.'

'Night-club!' He imitated me as he said it. 'Night-club! The sound of your voice tells me what you think. You are ashamed because I work in a night-club, but you don't know anything about it. You are quick to criticize my life, but you have no real knowledge of it.'

'Jeremy', I said, 'I'd like a calm discussion, please. You have accused me of being quick to criticize, but you mustn't think that I am entirely without sense. You cannot imagine that I would want to mix with the kind of people who go to this club of yours?'

'I'm sure you wouldn't,' he said angrily. 'You'd blame them for trying to enjoy themselves. You'd dislike them because they stay up late at nights and don't talk about living for others.'

I was becoming annoyed. 'Jeremy,' I said, 'you have decided to make fun of my ideas. Please remember that I am treating this discussion seriously.'

He groaned. 'It's happening just as I knew it would. *Why* do you have to question everything? *Why* do I have to give reasons and explain myself? What's wrong with leaving each other's private lives alone? Why can't we act in a friendly way to each other?'

'As your father,' I answered, 'I *cannot* take such an

attitude. The way you arrange your life must always affect me even if I am powerless to influence you.'

'That's what you say.' He leaned forward in his chair and looked at me angrily. 'I explain it differently. I think you are *afraid* of friendship with me. If you let us be friends you'd have to admit that there is some good in my ideas. You'd have to admit that I'd made a life of my own without the help of your principles. You've spent years hammering those principles into me – duty, discipline, and all the rest of them – but I can do without them. You'd have to admit that I'd escaped from the cage you built round me.'

I stood up. I was trembling and suddenly I felt very tired. I made a great effort and looked straight in his eyes, forcing myself to speak. 'I do not regret the way in which I brought you up. If I were to do it again I should not change it in any detail. You have come back after running away. When I ask you to explain yourself you tell me a story about a *club* and *jazz*. When I invite you to discuss your life with me you refuse to answer my questions. You dismiss with scorn the principles on which I have built my life.' I was so angry now that it was difficult to keep my voice steady, but I went on with my warning. 'At the moment, you are confident that your way of life is immensely better than mine. No advice will be of any use to you. But remember that you have only just started your independent life. You have a lot to learn. Don't regard me as an old fool with his head in the clouds. I know more than you think I do. For example, I know that you have placed yourself outside the law by avoiding national service. Your companions can hardly be honest men and women. You are treading a dangerous path. And you calmly propose that you and I should leave each other's private lives alone and be friends! No, Jeremy. If a man is not honest and upright, I can never be his friend, even if he is my own flesh and blood!'

As I stopped speaking, Jeremy lifted his head and looked about him. He looked first at me, then through the window at the garden, then round the room. It was as if he wanted to photograph every detail of the place in his memory before he left it.

'You're right,' he said at last. 'It was silly of me to come. I *have* chosen my own way and it *is* different from yours. I didn't think I was asking very much from you, but it seems it was too much. Of course your principles are more important to you than I am – it's one of your principles that they should be.'

He was silent for a moment; then he looked at me and said, 'So I'll go.' And before I could stop him he left the room. I heard the front door close and I saw him go past the garden hedge and away down the street.

Chapter 7
Sister and brother

While I was sitting in the kitchen I heard the front door shut and, of course, I knew that Jeremy had gone. For a moment I was tempted to run out of the house after him, but that would have done no good. He would only have thought that I was a silly old woman who understood nothing. So I sat in the kitchen waiting for my brother Alfred to do something.

I heard Alfred moving about as if he couldn't decide whether to come to me in the kitchen or go upstairs to his study. Please God, I thought, make him come in here to me. Don't let him go up to his study, away from me. Don't let him close his heart against me and never tell me what happened between him and Jeremy. Let him be angry with me if he must. Let him say wounding, terrible things to me, but don't let him shut himself away from me.

My prayer was answered. Alfred came into the kitchen. He hesitated as if he had forgotten what he wanted to say. His face was grey and he looked very old. Suddenly, I thought that he looked like a soldier, for he stood so straight although he was sad. I had never thought of him like that before, though I had seen him in his Army uniform during the First World War. Now, the thought came into my head: 'He is like a beaten general.'

It seemed as if he had heard my thoughts. He said, 'I'm beaten, Eleanor. There's nothing more that I can do.'

He spoke so quietly that I was ashamed of thinking that he might be angry. I felt full of pity for him.

'Beaten, Alfred?' I asked, as gently as I could. 'I don't understand.'

He turned his sad, grey face towards me. He was my own brother and I was unable to help him.

'We have to speak the truth to each other, Eleanor,' he said. 'Jeremy is my only son. I shall never have another. I did my best to bring him up in the right way. I tried to teach him to believe in duty and service to others. I wanted him to accept the principles by which my life had been governed. I have failed. He has just told me that my way of life means nothing to him. He refuses to accept my principles. He can do without them and he can do without me. I have failed, Eleanor. I have completely failed in my attempts to train his character. He regards me as a stupid old man, out of touch with real life and unable to understand anyone else's opinions.'

'And how do you regard him, Alfred?' I asked.

He shook his head. 'I don't know. I just don't know. He seems to have changed very little in some ways. He seems older. That is because he has taken some important decisions. Young people always seem older when they have done that. I don't know what he intends to do. I don't know on what principles he intends to build his life. He made little effort to explain himself to me. He probably thinks that I am not worth such an effort. He has finished with me.'

'Alfred dear,' I answered, 'I'm sure that Jeremy does not

hate you as his father. It isn't you that he has finished with. It's your principles – your way of life – that he has rejected.'

He looked at me with a flash of his old severe look. 'Eleanor,' he said, 'don't try to give me comfort with a false argument. If Jeremy rejects my principles – my way of life – he rejects me.'

'I don't see it that way at all.'

'Of course you don't, Eleanor.' He spoke gently, as if he were explaining something to a child. 'A man lives his life according to his principles. A woman depends on her instinct. Instinct will guide her, but instinct cannot guide a man. He must follow the principles that he believes in.'

'So because *you* believe in one set of principles and Jeremy believes in another, you can't live together in the same house!'

'No,' said Alfred. 'We can't. I am his father and it is my duty to try to influence him. He rejects my influence, so he has gone away.'

'And when shall we see him again? Did he say when he would come again?'

Alfred's face became hard. 'I don't know. I can't make plans for him,' he said.

Suddenly, I felt very lonely. 'Oh, Alfred,' I said, 'why did you let him go?'

'Could I keep him here by force?'

I began to cry. 'But he was here... you let him go... he has left us... we do not know where he is or what he will do...' I was crying too much to continue, but I heard Alfred's voice.

'We know something more important than that, my dear. We know what kind of life he has decided to follow. We know that he is on his own. I pray that he may be kept free from harm.'

'You pray!' I said. 'Don't be silly, Alfred. You don't believe in God.'

'No,' he answered, 'but you do. And perhaps your God

41

will keep him safe.'

We stood there in the kitchen, looking at each other and suddenly, for the first time in many years, we saw each other as sister and brother. It didn't make up for my terrible, aching sorrow about Jeremy, but it was something. It was much better than nothing. And it was all we had.

Chapter 8
Jeremy and Percy in Paris

I felt sad when I got out of the train in London. I was now completely cut off from my old life at home. I had failed to make my father understand me, and I had to get used to the idea. He hadn't made any effort to admit that my opinions might be right. He hadn't changed since I'd been away from home. If I didn't agree with him, he knew I was wrong – and that was that. So here I was, back in London, and my old life was over. I must forget it.

I settled down to my work again. Percy was away. He was sent to Scotland first and then, in June 1944, he was moved into France. During the last year of the war a lot of American soldiers visited the club and I learned from them about jazz experiments in the USA. I developed my own piano playing until I was able to play both 'old' and 'new' jazz. I saw Tim most nights. He was as cheerful as ever. Sometimes he had money; but usually he borrowed from his friends.

Then the war ended and everything happened at once. The American soldiers began to leave London to go home. Percy wrote a letter from Germany to say that he was being sent to America. From there, he was returning to Europe – to Paris. He asked me to form a jazz group in London and take them over to Paris where he would meet us in the New Year. The French, he said, were eager to hear good jazz again.

Well, I thought, why not? Why should I care whether I stayed in London or went to Paris? Paris was an attractive idea. I needed a change. If I stayed there for a few years the fact that I had avoided service in the Army would be forgotten. Most important, if I went to Paris, I'd be putting the English Channel between myself and the old man. I'd be turning away from my painful memories. I wouldn't be living in the same country as my father. The further away I went the better it would be for both of us.

I told Tim about my decision. I felt sorry to be leaving him, though I knew that he would soon forget me. He never thought about people when they weren't there. I remember wondering whether I could train myself to be like that.

When I told him about Paris, he laughed and rubbed his hands together. 'Paris?' he said. 'That will be fine for me. When do we start?'

'We?' I asked.

'Of course!' He smiled at me. 'You're not going there without a business manager. You trust your Uncle Tim, Jeremy. There are hundreds of ways in which I can be useful to you. You'll need me to look after your business interests. I'll see that you don't miss any opportunities.'

I knew that it was no use arguing. Tim was coming. He wasn't going to miss a chance like this.

Tim and I and the rest of the band got out of the train at the Gare du Nord on a cold January afternoon in 1946. Percy was waiting for us; and Paris was waiting for our jazz. The city was eager for the freedom that jazz represented. Like the other jazz bands playing in Paris then, we were more than entertainers. People enjoyed our music: that was what they came to the clubs to hear. But our kind of music represented a free spirit that Paris had almost forgotten during the war.

And, though it sounds like boasting, I can claim that we were worth hearing. Percy and I were experimenting all the time. We added the 'new' jazz to the 'old' – joined the two together and created a different music. We invented new sounds all the time and, in those exciting years in Paris, we never ran out of ideas.

I couldn't have succeeded without Percy, of course; but I began to realize that he depended on me too. We were building a new world for ourselves. It was such an interesting world that we didn't pay much attention to the real world outside it. We didn't notice that we were often cold and hungry. We discussed our music and practised during the day: we played every night. We never got tired and we never wanted a change.

Although I didn't realize it at the time, I was doing what my father had so often recommended to me: I was working hard and forgetting about myself. If anybody had told me that I was following one of my father's principles, I'd have laughed at the idea. I'd have pointed out that I was working hard at something that gave me delight. I'd have argued that the old man got little pleasure out of his work. He stopped doing a thing as soon as he began to enjoy it. He thought, I supposed, that he worked to make the world a better place. I worked to give pleasure to other people and to myself. Compared with him, I thought I was free. In fact, my life was spent in sleeping for about six hours of each day and working for the other eighteen. I never went anywhere and never met anyone unconnected with the work I had chosen to do. The old man himself never led a more disciplined life; but he *talked* about principles, and I didn't. If my father had been told in 1946 or 1947 that his son was one of the hardest-working people in Europe, he wouldn't have believed it. He wouldn't have agreed to the idea that a *jazz* musician working in *Paris* could be living a useful life. To him, Paris represented a time-wasting, pleasure-loving, selfish way of life.

But, for me, Paris was a magic world. It was *my* world. Say 'Paris' to me now, fifteen years later, and the magic

returns. I'm back there, with Percy and the other boys in the band. I'm sitting in the sun at midday, eating breakfast. There's no butter to put on the bread. The coffee is dark and bitter. There's a sharp, blue smell of French cigarettes and the sun is warm. I'm happy. Another day has come – a day on which Percy and I will play jazz. Soon, we'll be playing the greatest jazz in the world; and, meanwhile, the spirit of Paris floats us towards the future.

I said, a moment ago, that Percy had begun to depend on me. It was in the spring of 1947 that we realized that we were equal. Until then, I had been learning from him. Suddenly, we knew that we were exploring jazz together. We had always used my ideas as well as his, but he had always been a much better jazz player. Now, we both knew that my piano was as important to our music as his valve trombone. All the other players in the band knew this too. Percy welcomed this development. He was a warm-hearted, generous man, completely free from jealousy. The fact that my playing was now equal in quality to his seemed to make him like me more. Our friendship was built on trust and shared interests, but we didn't talk together very much – except about music, of course. I couldn't imagine what Percy's earlier life had been like, nor could he imagine mine. We had no memories to share, no common experiences to discuss. It was when we played our music together that we spoke directly to each other. Now that he was no longer leading me, Percy felt joy and relief. Through our jazz we now met and spoke as equal companions and the experience broke down his loneliness.

Percy had some friends, of course, apart from the other members of our band and me. Some of them were black American jazzmen like himself; others were French. He was learning the French language and reading about French life and history and politics. He always had a French newspaper sticking out of his pocket. Whenever he had a spare moment he would read it very slowly and seriously. Soon, he was very well-informed about France and the French people. He thought of France as *his* country. For the first time in his life Percy was a free citizen.

And so our lives went on. Percy was happy because of his music and his love of France. I was happy and proud to have become level with him as a jazzman. Our band played better and better and we made a reputation for ourselves.

Tim was happy too. Our success gave him a good life. He spent most of his time talking and drinking in the cafés and clubs of Paris. He didn't neglect his job. As our reputation climbed he found us fresh work. With his help, we changed clubs quite often and always went on to a better one. Tim knew everybody and he never missed a chance of getting more money for us.

He spent a lot of his time with Americans. He wanted to go to the States and he was determined to fix us up with a job there. He would, of course, go with us as our business manager. Tim believed that his quick tongue would bring him success in America. He may well have been right – and he certainly was a fast talker! I didn't see a lot of him at that time, but I knew that he was full of plans. When we did meet I was always glad to see him. He was always his cheerful, confident self. Sometimes I'd see him sitting outside a café with a drink in front of him and his arm round a girl. If he saw me he'd always wave and ask me to join him. 'Have a drink,' he'd say; and then he'd tell the story of the latest funny thing that had happened to him. Funny things were always happening to Tim. He was always in some kind of trouble but he never seemed to run out of luck.

One evening in September I saw him when he was really serious and business-like. I was walking past one of his favourite cafés when he rushed out and seized me by the arm. 'Come in,' he said. 'This is important.' He glanced quickly at me. 'Good,' he said, 'you've shaved, but you're not dressed too neatly. You look like a musician.'

'I *am* a musician,' I said, as he pulled me into the café. 'I don't have to look like one. What's your game?'

'Julius Walsheim,' he said. 'From New York. A big man in the American entertainment world. I've got him in here now. I've already sold him the idea of hiring you for an American tour. Come along in and smile, and we'll be in the States in thirty days' time.'

I knew this was important. All jazzmen need an American tour. A jazzman who hasn't been to the States is like a painter who hasn't been to Italy.

Tim led me to a table where a big man sat reading a newspaper. You didn't need to be told that he was an American. You could see at a glance that he was.

'We're in luck, Mr Walsheim,' said Tim, wearing a smile that stretched from ear to ear. 'Here's the jazzman that I was telling you about. Jeremy, this is Mr Walsheim.'

We shook hands. Mr Walsheim folded his newspaper and put it on the table. 'I've heard that you're quite a success in Paris, Mr Coleman. If you're interested in coming to the States, I think maybe we could fix up something between the two of us.'

'I'm interested,' I answered, 'but I'm under contract with my present club and I can't sign an agreement that breaks my contract.'

Tim trod softly on my toe under the table. 'I've just been telling Mr Walsheim that the band is free whenever he wants us.'

Mr Walsheim fixed his dark eyes on me. 'What was that you were saying, Mr Coleman?' he asked. He was as serious as a priest.

I didn't try to make excuses for Tim. Walsheim obviously liked straight talking. 'I said that I didn't want to break our contract with our present club.'

Mr Walsheim glanced at Tim. Then he looked at me and smiled. 'I like to hear that,' he said. 'I never sign an agreement with any band that has a reputation for breaking contracts.'

'Breaking contracts?' Tim cried out. 'Who's talking about breaking contracts? Our agreement with the club isn't in writing. The manager of the club and I arrived at an understanding during a business conversation. There's nothing written down.'

I knew that he probably had the written contract in his pocket, but I said nothing. I had to let him try to regain Walsheim's good opinion.

Walsheim paid no attention to Tim's words. 'I know the manager of your club, Mr Coleman,' he said. 'I'll come along tonight to hear you play. If I like what I hear, you and I can maybe do a little business.'

He paid for his drink and Tim's, picked up his newspaper, and gave me a friendly nod. Then he walked out into the street.

Tim seized my hand and waved it up and down. 'You see?' he shouted. 'You're in safe hands, my boy. Leave it all to Uncle Tim. We've won! Walsheim will go wild with excitement when he hears the band.'

I couldn't imagine Mr Walsheim going wild in any conditions, but I was astonished at Tim's self-congratulations. 'You nearly ruined everything,' I said.

'I *what*? Listen, I had to follow him about for hours to get a chance to talk to him. I'd heard he was in Paris and I telephoned his hotel, but he wouldn't give me an appointment. I've *worked* for this success, my boy.'

He was so pleased with himself that I said no more about his foolish lies about our contract with the club. He talked happily about the great time we were going to have in the States. We had a drink and a few good laughs. When I left him I felt certain that we had, after all, a good business manager.

I didn't tell any of the boys that Mr Walsheim would be listening to the band that night. Great things depended on their playing and I didn't want to make them nervous. We just played as usual, neither better nor worse. I watched Walsheim. He didn't seem to be listening to us. He wandered about the club, watching people as they came and went. So I decided to forget about him and just play. If he liked it, good. If not, why worry? We could stay in Paris for a lot longer without feeling sorry for ourselves.

We finished at about four o'clock in the morning. I was just getting my coat, ready to go home, when Walsheim tapped me on the shoulder. 'Well, Mr Coleman,' he said, smiling at me, 'I've spoken to the manager here. He'll be sorry to lose you after Christmas, but if you want to come to the States, he won't argue.'

He put on a grey overcoat and took his hat from the hook. 'We can agree on the details of your contract later,' he said. 'I shall want you to sign an agreement to make records for my company.'

'I can't do anything without my business manager,' I answered, looking round for Tim.

Walsheim smiled, as if I were having a joke with him. 'I'm not sure that he knows much about that kind of contract,' he said. 'But don't worry. I shan't try to cheat you.'

'But you didn't listen to our music,' I said.

He smiled again. 'In my business, Mr Coleman, you don't listen to the music. You watch the customers.' And he looked at me as if to say, 'Now you understand why I'm rich.'

He went. I was alone in the club. I was successful. We were all successful. We were going to be famous and very rich. Percy was going back, famous and rich, to the country where he'd been ill-treated and poor. I knew that everything in my life had been a preparation for this moment.

The next morning I got up early. It wasn't twelve o'clock

when I climbed out of bed. I wanted to see Percy and tell him the great news. I hadn't finished dressing when Tim tapped at my door and rushed in.

'Congratulations!' he shouted. 'I've fixed everything. I've been to Walsheim's hotel. He thought that you and the boys were great.'

I didn't tell him what Walsheim had said last night. I wanted Tim to have his share of the fun.

'Did he sign a contract this morning?' I asked.

Tim paused. 'Well – no. I didn't actually see him. I spoke to him on the telephone in his room from the hotel desk downstairs. He wants to talk to you about the details of the contract.'

'Shouldn't you be there when we talk?' I asked. I could see that Walsheim had brushed Tim aside. 'After all, you are our business manager and you shouldn't trust me to make arrangements about contracts and money.' I wanted to hear what he would say.

He tapped me on the shoulder, smiling happily. 'I've got complete confidence in you, Jeremy, my boy. My job is to fix things up in broad general outline. I've done that; and now I leave you to attend to the details.'

I laughed. I had to admire his spirit. Nobody could have guessed from the way he looked and spoke that Walsheim had defeated him.

I got rid of him before I hurried off to see Percy. This was going to be a big moment and I didn't want Tim there.

Percy had just got up. He was sitting by the open window, drinking coffee. The sun shone in – it was a perfect autumn day – and Percy looked very comfortable and happy. I felt wonderfully glad that I was going to make him even happier.

He fetched me a cup and poured out some more coffee. I sat down in the sunshine, enjoying the whole lovely situation.

'Percy,' I said, letting him have the news bit by bit.

'We're going to make some records.'

'We are?' he said, turning to me with a round-eyed stare. 'What happened? How did you fix it up?'

I told him that Walsheim wanted us to make some records for his company. He was just as pleased and excited as I'd hoped he would be. Immediately, his mind started working on the music we should record and the musicians we should use.

'I think we need a different drummer for recording,' he said. 'Doug's too heavy. Have you noticed? He's good but, man, he's *heavy*.'

He went on talking, and I sat back. Then I interrupted him. 'That's not all my news. That's just part of it.'

'Huh?'

'The records are part of a larger contract that Walsheim is offering us. He's going to provide us with steady work and take us all over there.'

Percy put down his coffee cup. 'Over where?' he asked.

I laughed. 'To the States, of course. To America. Don't you want to go home?'

There was a long silence – and then he said, 'No.'

'But...' I said, and stopped.

'I want to stay here,' said Percy. He looked at me and I saw that his eyes were very sad. 'You must go, Jeremy. It's very important for you. You need it. You'll meet a lot of people over there, a lot of great jazzmen who can teach you things.'

'I won't go without you, of course!' I said, fiercely.

Percy shook his head. 'You must,' he said. 'You can't get ahead any more without going over there. I can get a job in Paris. There's plenty of work for me to do here.'

'I'm not denying that,' I said. 'I'm saying that I'm not going without you.'

'Why not?' he asked quietly.

'To begin with,' I said, 'Walsheim isn't just hiring me. He's hiring the band and without you the band wouldn't exist.'

Percy shook his head again. 'You could build it up. You're good enough now to do that. You'll find plenty of trumpet or trombone players who'll be glad to work with you.'

'But Percy,' I said, 'I don't understand. *Why* don't you want to come?'

He went very quiet, looking at me as a king might look at one of his ministers who was being a nuisance. 'A man's got to go his own way,' he said, at last. 'I know where I'm going, and it's not to the United States.'

'All right, Percy,' I said. 'I'll tell Walsheim we're not going.'

'You're crazy,' he answered. 'You've got to get over there, sooner or later – every jazzman must. Don't be crazy! What am I, your *nurse*? You go and play jazz in the States for two or three years. You'll find me here in Paris when you want to join up with me again.'

It was a fair offer. Jazzmen are always splitting up and coming together again. I can't think why I was so upset about it. I suppose I'd been so excited about going to the States that Percy's refusal hurt me. I couldn't understand why he refused to go. Also, his remark about his being my nurse stung me. I'd always felt small compared with him – and now he was making me feel smaller than ever.'

'No,' I said. 'Either you can come, or I don't go.'

'You're crazy,' was all he said.

I didn't know what else to say, so I said nothing. I just turned and went out leaving Percy sitting there, pouring himself another cup of coffee.

I went and walked in the Luxembourg Gardens. The sun shone and the paths were thickly covered with autumn leaves. People were sitting about – young lovers, and mothers with little children – and the garden was very quiet in the midday sun. I suddenly realized how much I loved

Paris. I was at home there. And yet Percy was right to tell me to go and get some experience in America. He was also right not to want to move away from Paris. He loved it, too. It was his home, now. After all, America was nothing new to him. He already knew all it had to teach him about music.

'You're too comfortable, boy,' I said to myself. 'Do as Percy says. Go over to the States and make yourself famous.'

An old man passed by, carrying a long loaf of bread. He had a little silver-coloured beard and a black hat. He looked wonderful. All old men look wonderful in France. I suppose it's because they're not ashamed of being old. As I watched him walk by I thought how much I liked being in France. I had no wish to leave it – ever. But suddenly, I saw Percy's face and I heard his scornful question: 'What am I, your *nurse*?' And I got up off the chair, knowing what I was going to do. I was going to the States. I'd stay there three or four years, whether I liked it or not. I'd learn all the time, work hard all the time, play my very best. I'd take every opportunity of playing with people better than myself. I was going to the top of the jazz world if hard work could take me there. Then I'd come back to Paris and find Percy and we'd get a band going. We'd play jazz in Paris for the rest of our lives.

I believed in myself again. The autumn air and the warm sun flowed through my body. I was confident that I could stand alone. I still liked Percy; still admired him; but I did not depend on him any longer. I was going to America and when I returned I would make Percy an offer he could not refuse.

Chapter 9
Goodbye Tim

When I arrived at the club that evening Tim was waiting for me. His American friends had heard that we were going to the States and they had decided to give a big party. Tim said that I had to go the party as soon as I could manage to leave the band. I felt like a party, so I telephoned Lou de Rogiero, a good jazz pianist. He couldn't keep a regular job because he drank too much, but he really could play. He helped me whenever he could. At about midnight I told him to carry on and I left the club, determined to celebrate.

I took a taxi to the address that Tim had given me. It was a big flat in a very expensive district of Paris. As I went in, the noise told me that the guests were really celebrating. In the middle of a big room full of people I found Tim. He was talking to a very pretty American girl, but he said hello and smiled at me and introduced me to her. It was her flat and she was giving the party. She wasn't only pretty, she was obviously very rich, too. Tim wasn't pleased that she liked me more than she liked him. But I was celebrating and I couldn't worry too much about him. He wandered off and found another girl to talk to. I sat drinking and talking happily to my pretty American until the party ended and it was time to go home.

I'd been asleep for only about three hours when there was a knocking at my bedroom door. Waking up was horrible. I had a terrible headache. 'I'm coming,' I shouted; and I walked very slowly and carefully into my sitting room.

The French woman from whom I rented my flat was standing there. Beside her stood a tall, fair young woman and two little children. The fair young woman looked very sad and tired.

'M'sieu Coleman,' said Madame Leroux, 'you 'ave visitors.' Then she went out shutting the door hard behind her. The noise split my head open.

'I'm very sorry about this, Mr Coleman,' said my unexpected visitor. 'I *had* to find you. I've been here three or four times, but you were out each time I came. I'm sorry to arrive so early in the morning, but I *must* talk to you.'

I made a big effort and gave her my attention. She was about thirty, I suppose, and still very good-looking, but she was tired and worried. She was in need of a holiday and some fun. The children were very quiet and stayed close to their mother. The girl looked about five and the boy about three.

'I'm here to ask you not to take Tim to America,' she said. 'I'm his wife.'

I wasn't surprised. Somehow, I'd known who she was.

'He left us behind in London when he came to Paris with you,' she said. 'He didn't tell me where he was going. I discovered where he was and I borrowed the money to come here. He doesn't send us any money, you see. Tim just disappears when he wants to. Then he comes back, smiling, as if he'd never been away at all.'

'And you let him come back to live with you?'

'I have done – twice. But I won't have him back again. Not this time. I've come to Paris to tell him that I've finished with him. But he's left me with two children and I must get some money from him. He's their father. He ought to help me to support them. If he goes to America I'll never get any help from him.'

'Listen,' I said, 'I was out very late last night and I drank too much. I've got a terrible headache and I can't think very clearly. I promise that I'll help you and I won't take Tim to America or anywhere else. Now, will you please make some coffee for us while I go and get dressed?'

'Of course,' she said, calmly, and went towards the gas stove. I returned to my bedroom and began to put on my clothes. My headache was worse when I moved fast, so I didn't hurry. In any case, I wanted to think. I didn't like the idea of what I'd got to do. I was fond of Tim but I wasn't going to help him to cheat his wife and children. It wasn't going to be easy. Tim had been part of my life for some years. He had influenced me in many ways and it was a shock to discover how badly he had behaved. I had to ask myself whether I had been cheating and lying, too.

I finished dressing and went back into the sitting room. We drank coffee and I began to feel better. Tim's wife told me that her name was Jane. The little girl was called Belinda and the boy was called Timothy.

He had been named after his father – the father who had walked away from him and his sister and his mother.

'We must go round to Tim's hotel at once,' I said. I sounded a lot more confident than I felt. 'He won't have got up yet. We'll make him admit that he must look after you all and we'll collect some money off him. I'll tell him that he's not coming to America with me. It won't be a nice meeting, but we've got to do it. In any case, it'll be worse for him than for us.'

Jane shook her head. 'I wouldn't be too sure of that,' she said. 'Tim won't be ashamed of himself. He'll be surprised for the first minute or two, but he'll soon recover. As a matter of fact, I don't think he'll even be surprised. He knows that I know that he's in Paris. He must have been expecting me to turn up sometime.'

'Has he written to you?'

She shook her head again. 'Oh, no. Tim doesn't write letters. When he disappears, he disappears without trace. Then he comes back and acts as if nothing had happened. He lives from moment to moment as if he had no memory of his own actions.'

I saw what she meant. She was describing the Tim I knew. I had admired him for living his life entirely in the present. His way of life was so different from my father's.

It was so completely different from the way I had been brought up. Tim never talked about principles and duty and living for others. And was this the result? Was this what happened when you lived like Tim?

'Well, let's go,' I said. 'I want to get this over.' I hated what I'd got to do. I liked Jane and I was sorry for her. I was angry with Tim for what he had done to her and his children. But I wanted to get out of their affairs as quickly as possible. I wanted to be by myself and to think.

I took a taxi and we sat in it silently, watching the grey streets and the dirty, unpainted buildings. Tim lived about two miles away. Suddenly, I heard a soft noise and I realized that Jane was crying. My heart sank.

'Don't,' I said. 'Please don't.' And I took her hand in mine.

She tried to smile. 'I'm sorry,' she said. 'I can't – ' And she cried harder. Of course, both the children cried too. And the taxi stopped. The driver looked at me as if it was all my fault.

'C'est ça,' he said in a nasty voice.

'We're here,' I said to Jane. I got the three of them out of the taxi and it drove away. 'Now,' I said, 'go into that café across the street, Jane, and buy yourself a strong drink. Get the children some chocolate. Here's some money. When you've dried your eyes and are feeling better, come back here.' I pointed out the little hotel where Tim lived. 'Knock on the door of room number twenty-seven. Tim and I will be in there.'

She took the money I held out to her. 'Thank you,' she said. 'Can you give me ten minutes? I'll be better then.'

'I'll give you ten minutes,' I answered. And I watched her walk into the café before I entered the hotel. Outside Tim's room I paused. My heart was beating loudly. I knocked. There was no answer, so I walked in.

Tim was in bed; and there was a girl in bed with him. It was the girl I'd seen him talking to at the party. They were both asleep.

'Oh, God!' I thought, 'he *would*! And Jane and the children will be here in a few minutes.'

I shook the girl. 'Come on!' I said. 'The party's over! Dress yourself and get out of here fast.'

'Who the hell are you?' She looked at me as if she could have killed me. But she did as she was told and disappeared without asking any more questions.

Tim struggled to wake up. He looked terrible. He probably felt terrible, too. 'Hey!' he said. 'What's up with you? Why did you send her out? Can't we talk without – ?'

'Shut up!' I commanded. I could hear Jane's footsteps on the stairs and the voices of Tim's children. I opened the door and they came into the room.

Tim opened his eyes wide and sat up in bed. He opened his mouth as if to speak, then shut it again.

'So this is where you live, Tim,' said Jane. 'It's a good thing that I don't intend to live with you, isn't it? There's not much room here for me and the children.'

'Oh, I'll take care of you, darling,' said Tim. As usual, he thought fast. 'As a matter of fact, I've been looking at one or two houses that we can live in when I bring you over to Paris. It's not easy to buy a house here. Jeremy will tell you that, but I think I've found one. We'll soon have a home here and, in any case, I'm very glad to see you.'

'A home in Paris?' Jane asked. 'I thought you were going to America!'

'Oh, yes!' said Tim. 'I was forgetting. I'm not properly awake yet, darling. Sit down while I get dressed and then we'll go out for some food.'

'It's all right, Tim,' Jane interrupted him. 'You needn't talk nonsense. I've finished with you; and you'll never see your children again, so have a good look at them now. I just want some *money* from you. Do you hear? I had to borrow the money to come to Paris to find you. There's no money to feed your children or to buy them clothes. Do you understand? I want *money* to take care of your children. It doesn't matter where it comes from. Borrow it from your girl-friends if you like to.'

The two children obviously didn't understand what was happening, but they knew that their mother was upset. They began to cry. While Jane spoke to them and dried their eyes, Tim looked at me with a half smile on his face. 'These little troubles!' he seemed to be saying. 'She *would* turn up here with the children just after I've been drinking too much and I'm not thinking very clearly.' As usual, he was carrying on as if nothing serious had happened.
But I wasn't going to help him. Jane's arrival in Paris with the children had made me see things differently. There was nothing to admire in Tim's behaviour. I'd finished with him. Before I said goodbye to him I'd do what I could to help Jane.

'Tim,' I said, 'you can forget about America and you can forget about Paris, too. You aren't working with my band any longer. I don't suppose anything will *force* you to go back home and support your family, but I'm not going to help you to avoid your responsibilities.' I realized afterwards that I must have sounded just like my father!

'Don't get so excited!' he said. 'Jane's been like this before. She needs a little time. She'll see everything differently when I've had a chance to talk to her. You needn't interfere.'

'Oh, stop being such a fool,' I answered roughly. 'Jane's told you. She's finished with you. She's determined to make you support your children, but that's the end. Now, how much money have you got here?'

I picked up a handful of coins lying on the dressing table. 'Here! Put that down!' he shouted, coming towards me. A cold, cruel anger flowed through me. I raised my arm to hit him, but he sank down on the bed again. He looked terribly tired and puzzled.

'There's not much here,' I said. 'Where's the rest?'

'That's all I've got.'

'Very well,' I said. 'We'll take the rest in goods. And I picked up his watch and put it in my pocket. I thought he would attack me again, but he changed his mind.

An astonishing scene followed. The children were crying again and Jane was trying to keep them quiet. I searched the room, packing into suitcases everything that was worth selling. Jane wasn't going back to England with empty hands if I could help her. And Tim sat there on the bed, watching me and saying nothing.

I took his silk shirts and his best suit and a good pair of shoes and his electric razor. I left him with one old suit to wear but, apart from that, I cleaned him out of his possessions.

'Come on,' I said to Jane. 'We've got all there is to get. Now you'll have to find a lawyer to deal with him. My guess is that he'll disappear without leaving his address.'

'Of course he will,' she said, 'but at least we've got something to be going on with.'

Tim just sat there and watched us go. He didn't look like a real person to me any longer. I think that he realized that his marriage to Jane was over. He had almost forgotten it before we reached the door. You couldn't really touch Tim's heart. He hadn't any loyalty to anyone.

I sold all his property and took the money to Jane at her hotel. She was very grateful, and we sat and talked about her plans. She intended to return to England at once and get on with her job. She wasn't hopeful that Tim would send her any money for the children. She was just relieved that she had finished with him at last. As I listened, I realized again how wrong I'd been about Tim when I first knew him. Oh yes, he was amusing. He was a light-hearted and interesting companion. But he couldn't be trusted. He *used* people. When he couldn't use them any more, he threw them away.

It was time for me to go. I liked Jane. I didn't want to

get too fond of her. I couldn't help her any more than I had done already. I couldn't help anyone, for I had a lot to learn about myself.

One is often slow to realize things. For several days I didn't realize how completely I had ended that particular chapter of my life. I went along to the club each night, as usual, and I played. I played badly. After three bad nights I told Percy that I needed a rest. Lou de Rogiero played the piano for the band in place of me.

Percy and I didn't talk about America again. He hadn't changed his mind. I had lost my wish to go. Going to America had been necessary for my music, but my life had crashed and my music with it. I just couldn't go on. I felt as if everything I had been doing had been a lie – either a lie or a mistake, it didn't matter which. I had been trying to live for the moment. I had been trying to be Tim. Now that I saw how impossible it was to be Tim, I didn't know who to be. I felt that I'd like to be Jeremy – but I didn't know who Jeremy was. I had to find a new life and I hoped to find myself.

I had to get away from everything and everyone – even Percy. So I packed my few possessions and went back to England. I couldn't stay in Paris any longer, and London was the only other city where I knew I could make a living.

I wrote to Percy and told him that I'd finished with the band. I said I hoped that he would carry on with it. I wished him luck.

He sent me a letter back, asking what was up. I didn't answer. I needed to be alone. I needed a quiet life. I had to think. I had to discover who and what Jeremy Coleman was.

Chapter 10
Jeremy finds himself at last

The period of my life that I'm now describing lasted ten years. It's hard for me to believe it now, but it's true. In most people's lives there are periods in which nothing seems to happen. There's no development. Then, suddenly, something definite happens and life takes a new shape. That's how my life went between 1948 and 1958. All that happened was that I became ten years older. My soul – the real *me* – was asleep.

My music didn't develop because nobody wanted it to. Those ten years were the worst period in the history of jazz. Nobody wanted it. The 'new' jazz stayed 'new'. Very few people listened to it. The 'old' jazz stayed 'old'. It had its followers but it didn't make progress. Percy and I had dreamed of uniting the old and the new. We were going to create a new art out of the two. But I had lost Percy and I had lost my vision of art. A lot of jazzmen gave up the struggle in those wasted years. A horrible kind of popular music conquered the world of entertainment. It was a deafening noise called 'rock-and-roll' – and it nearly killed jazz.

But I mustn't make excuses. I didn't try very hard during those years. Nothing seemed worth the effort. I made a living. My years in Paris with Percy had give me a reputation and it was easy for me to find work in various clubs as a jazz pianist. I made a few records and I was on the radio several times. I didn't make a lot of money but I had enough for my needs. I didn't think much about the future.

I came to life again at last – as I had to – through music: through music and the memory of a friendship. I was on my way to work one evening when I saw an advertisement for a jazz band. 'The Percy Brett Band', the advertisement stated, would perform in a big London theatre. I walked on. So Percy had his own band now. Well, naturally, he would. And, naturally, he hadn't told me about it. Why should he? I hadn't kept in touch with him, and I wouldn't be good enough to play with him now. My music had been standing still. I hadn't improved. I'd lost the desire to invent. Had his music developed? Had he left me far behind him?

Suddenly I knew that I *had* to hear Percy's band. Who was playing the piano for him? Had he managed to find someone who could work with him as I used to?

I went down the steps into the club, hung up my overcoat, and sat down at the piano. And I said 'Percy', aloud. 'Percy, this is for you.' And I played as I hadn't done for years. I put my heart into it; and I put my brain into it, too. As I was playing I was thinking. Thinking about music, I mean. Ideas flashed from my brain to my fingers. I kept on imagining that Percy was standing beside me, with that wonderful valve-trombone of his, waiting to join in.

After about forty minutes I let my hands drop from the keys. The regular members of the club had gathered round the piano. 'Hey, that was great!' one of them said. 'That was really *great*! We haven't heard you play like that for a long time. Have a drink with me.'

'Thanks,' I said. I raised the glass. 'Here's luck to what I used to be!' I said. I still couldn't believe that anything had changed.

I arrived at the theatre early so that I got a good seat, and I waited as patiently as I could. At last, Percy walked on to the stage, his trombone under his arm. He was chatting quietly to the white man who walked on with him. They seemed to be saying something about the music, because the white man sat down at the piano and played a few chords. Percy nodded, put his horn to his lips and blew a passage. The pianist nodded in his turn and played again. They stopped; ran through the passage again; then nodded at each other, as if they were now satisfied that it was right. All this happened while the rest of the band were coming on stage and arranging themselves.

A wave of misery broke over me. I had expected to suffer, but I had not expected to suffer as much as I was doing. I was full of envy. *I* should have been sitting at that piano. *I* should have been talking to Percy. *We* should have been discussing *our* ideas about the music that we were going to play. The pianist had a long, intelligent face. He looked like a hard worker; and I *hated* him! He'd got the job that I had thrown away. He was playing music with Percy. And he was probably a better musician than I had ever been.

Then they started playing; and I knew at once that Percy had progressed. He'd moved on; he'd gone on with our dream. They were playing *his* jazz. I knew, too, that he'd gone on alone. The other musicians in his band were good, but they were no better than plenty of other jazzmen I knew. The pianist wasn't better than I was. He wasn't nearly as good as I *could* have been. He wasn't as good as I still *could* be. It was a good performance, but it was nothing compared with what Percy and I could have done if we'd gone on working together.

Percy looked older – and wiser. The years had left their mark on him. He'd grown a beard. He'd put on weight and his head sat very squarely on his immense shoulders. He played with enormous power, and was in complete command of the band. He had to be – they were not equal to him.

As I listened, I knew what I had lost. I was years behind Percy in skill but I was equal to him in imagination. My fingers tapped the back of the seat in front of me. As Percy played, I played with him. Silently, I supplied the piano sounds that he needed to carry him smoothly from one musical idea to the next. For the whole of that evening Percy and I played together, but the music that we made was never heard.

When it was over I hesitated. Should I go to see him or not? I knew that he would welcome me. Percy was easy and natural in any awkward situation. Now that he was in London again after all these years, he might wonder why I didn't come forward and greet him. But I hesitated and, in the end, I didn't go. We had separated. Our old life was over. What could we say to each other?

I'd seen Percy, so I'd satisfied my curiosity. He was moving forward. I was standing still. I didn't quarrel with my life so long as I was left alone. Every evening I arrived at the club and played the piano for five or six hours. I didn't play badly, and the customers never complained; but I knew how much better I could have been. I just didn't care any longer.

Our evening, as I sat at the piano, playing but not thinking very much, I realized that the customers were all looking towards the stage. They seemed to be waiting for something to happen. I turned my head and tried to look behind me. As I did so, I heard a noise that I had thought I would never hear again. I heard the notes of Percy's horn weaving in and out of my music. I turned back to the piano and I began to play as I had not played for years. I could not see Percy, but his music drove me on. The notes of his trombone rose and fell, insisting that I did my best. My tired playing of the last few years would not satisfy Percy.

As I played, my mind was busy. So, I thought, Percy had found me. I had hidden myself away from him, but here he was. He was approaching me through music and not through words. He had crept on to the stage while I was bending over the piano keys and could not see him. We were talking to each other in our language. Through our music we could tell each other the truth.

And I kept on playing. I knew that I was drawing Percy's best music out of him. Then, after about a quarter of an hour, his horn played softly and I knew that he was waiting for me to lead. I was afraid. I might not be good enough. I might fail him. I turned and looked at him for the first time. He stood there and waited. He smiled and nodded at me. 'Play, man!' he called. 'Take over! Go!' And the club members standing round the stage shouted, 'Go, Jeremy! Go!'

For almost the first time in ten years, my hands hit the keys as if they wanted to. When I was a boy at home I had escaped from my prison through jazz. It was the same again now. The prison was different. It was no longer a prison that my father had built for me. It was a prison that I had built for myself – the prison of my dying imagination and my dead music. But now, I was alive again. I was free – I was rescued – by music.

Sweat poured off me. My piano sang. I could hear the fans clapping and shouting. When Percy joined in again they went wild with delight. We kept it up for about half an hour, and then, with a last great crash of music, we dived into silence.

Percy and I went over to the bar. He smiled and lifted his beer-glass to his lips in his own special way. As I watched him, the wasted years disappeared.

'Percy,' I said, 'tell me if I'm still alive.'

He laughed aloud – and his laugh was just the same as ever. 'Alive? I don't know. But I think you will live!'

'You'll help me?' I asked.

All he said was, 'When do we start?'

Percy and his band were in England for a nine-week tour, playing in theatres and clubs all over the country. At the end of the tour, most of his musicians were going back to Paris. Percy would be free then to make his own plans.

Ted, his drummer, was keen to stay with Percy and he seemed to like the idea of joining up with me. I knew most of the jazzmen in London, so we arranged that I'd collect a band together while Percy and Ted were away on their tour. We needed three more men to complete the band: a trumpeter, a guitar player and a bass-player. I was confident that I could find three really good jazzmen to fill those places.

I went to the railway station with Percy when he and Ted left London. We were both full of happiness and confidence. Everything seemed possible. The years we had spent apart didn't matter any more.

'I can hear it, man, already.' Percy shook my hand just as he had done when I first saw him off at a railway station. That had been in war-time London on the first night we met. 'I can hear it,' he said. 'The great music we'll make. The music of Jeremy Coleman and his band.'

'You mean Percy Brett and his band,' I said.

Percy shook his head. 'No, Jeremy, I don't. I've had years of being in front of a band. I play better when I'm working in somebody else's band.'

I tried to persuade him to change his mind, but he wouldn't. Perhaps he meant just what he said. Perhaps he thought that having my own band again would be good for me and give me confidence. I never knew the answer. There were things that Percy kept to himself.

The time passed slowly at first, but I had a lot to do. I chose the three jazzmen that we needed. That took a lot of time and thought. I couldn't afford to make mistakes. I chose an agent to deal with the band's business affairs. His job was to arrange tours for us and to bargain for our professional fees. It wasn't easy. Rock-and-roll ruled the entertainment world. Very few people seemed willing to pay fees to hire a jazz band. Managers of theatres and clubs were afraid of risking money by hiring us to play. They were not sure of getting audiences to listen to us.

I didn't worry. We wanted to play good jazz. That was all we wanted to do. We'd be content with very little money so long as we could play our music.

At last, I got a letter from Percy telling me the exact date of his return to London. He'd be back on March 5 and he'd arrive at Paddington Station at 11.30 pm.

Then I was really busy, preparing a welcome for him. I planned a big party – a very special kind of party. Percy's return to London and the first performance of my new band were going to take place at the same time.

I hired a big room near Paddington Station. I bought plenty of drink. I invited a lot of guests – all jazz fans. I arranged for our musicians to be there. Percy was going to meet his fellow-jazzmen as soon as he got back. He was going to get to know them by talking his own language to them – the language of his wonderful trombone.

That party occupied all my thoughts for weeks. I hadn't looked forward to anything so much since I was a child. When March 5 at last arrived I spent the whole day checking over my arrangements to make sure that nothing could go wrong.

Eleven o'clock came, and I took a taxi to Paddington. Long before Percy's train was due I was standing on the platform, waiting for it. This was the great night! I was eager to start playing. Percy would be tired at first, but he'd have a few drinks and listen to us. Then, I knew, he'd pick up that horn and join us in the music.

It was a wonderful night. Even in Paddington you knew that it was spring. Life was starting all over again. And then, Percy's train came in. I saw his great square form at the end of the platform. He had a big bag in one hand and his trombone-case in the other. He saw me at once and called my name. He was bare-headed, and the station lights were reflected in his broad, shining, black face.

'Man!' he said. '*Man*! I'm glad to be back. That hall we've just been playing in – '

'Tell me all about it in the taxi,' I said. I was as excited as a schoolboy and I couldn't waste time. Percy wanted to know where we were going, but I wouldn't tell him anything. I said that I'd got a little surprise for him. I knew it was childish, but I wanted to see his face when he walked into the room. He'd see all those musicians with their instruments, and all those drinks. He'd be surrounded by the whole wonderful atmosphere of welcome – and he'd know that it was all arranged for him.

The party room was in a house in a very quiet street. The taxi stopped nearby and I got out and paid the driver. Percy unloaded his bag and his trombone case and I turned round to pick up his bag. I didn't carry it far. Half a dozen fellows were standing round the steps of the house we had been going to enter. Whether they knew we were coming or whether they just happened to be there, I didn't know then and I don't know now. I dropped the bag and stared at them.

Two of them stood directly in front of Percy, blocking his way. They were smiling cruelly into his face. They were ugly, violent men, eager for trouble. Percy stood square and upright. His head moved slowly from side to side as he looked first at the two and then at the other four behind them.

Then I heard his voice. 'You fellows looking for somebody?'

For an instant there was silence. The other four moved closer, but nobody spoke. Then, one of them said slowly, in a thin voice, 'We're looking for somebody. We're looking for black men.'

'That's right,' said the other. 'We're looking for niggers. It looks as if we've found one. You're a nigger, ain't yer?'

They were enjoying themselves. They were in no hurry to start beating Percy. One of them produced a razor and opened it slowly.

My heart was thundering and I was covered with sweat. I wanted to run away. I wanted to run for the police. I wanted to be anywhere except where I was. But I couldn't even turn my head to see if there was any help in sight.

And I heard Percy's voice again. It was calm and level. 'Yes,' he said, 'I'm a black man, all right. I'm what you call a nigger. And you are a yellow pig who isn't fit to clean my shoes.'

Then, I knew it was coming; and I moved up to Percy's side. And as I stood by him, they rushed.

Chapter 11
Father and son

I was conscious when they picked us up and put us in the ambulance. I learned afterwards that our taxi-driver saw the six men attack us. He drove to the nearest telephone box and rang the police and the ambulance service. He didn't get mixed up in the fight, but he probably saved our lives.

I was conscious, as I say; and I knew that Percy was in the ambulance, too. When we reached Paddington General Hospital, I became unconscious for several hours. When I woke up I didn't understand very much for a few days. I just lay on my back, feeling sorry for myself. I had several broken bones and a razor-cut across my upper lip. It was painful to breathe, to eat, or to talk. They had kicked me in the face and all over my body.

I was told that Percy was in another part of the hospital. His wounds were more serious than mine. He had more broken bones and was in need of extra care. They told me that he had been asking to see me and that, when we were both recovering, we'd be allowed to meet.

I blamed myself for having led Percy into danger, though the attack could have happened in any of the violent areas of London. It was a bad time. There were frequent fights between black people and white people in the poor districts, but I hadn't realized that we might be attacked. Percy and I were friends and I had paid very little attention to race problems.

The nurses told me that my aunt had telephoned the hospital several times to ask how I was. She had told the hospital that she had read about Percy and me in the newspapers. 'You'll be having a visitor soon,' the nurses informed me.

'Dear Aunt Eleanor,' I thought, 'it must have been a shock for you. You'd hardly be able to believe that such a terrible thing could happen to the little boy you brought up.' I smiled at the thought of her. Then I stopped smiling because it hurt.

One afternoon, I was lying half asleep, when a tall figure came into my line of vision. It was a man, walking stiffly, and making straight for my bed. It couldn't be! It wasn't possible! But it was...it was the old man! I was so surprised that I didn't say anything. I didn't even ask him to sit down. He looked terrible. He looked hundreds of years older than when I had last seen him. He stood by my bedside, looking at me as if he didn't recognize me.

At last, I said, 'Hello, Dad. Sit down, won't you?'

He sat down, still looking at me in that distant way. He seemed to be very old and very tired.

'Jeremy, my boy,' he said, 'it's strange to see you here.'

'Well,' I said, 'people do generally go to hospital when they have their bones broken.'

'Ah, yes!' he answered. 'Yes, of course. It was your aunt who read about this unfortunate affair in the newspapers. She insisted that I came to see you.'

'So that's it,' I thought. 'You wouldn't have come unless she'd made you.' But I kept my thoughts to myself and said nothing.

'To tell you the truth,' he went on, 'I find it all very strange. I haven't been inside a hospital for a great many years.'

'Really?' I said. I wasn't very interested, but if he wanted to talk about hospitals I wasn't going to stop him. It was going to be hard enough to find subjects for conversation.

'The last time I was in hospital was nearly forty years ago, Jeremy,' the old man continued. 'It was an army hospital in France; near Arras, I think, though I was very confused when I was taken there. I wasn't there long; my wounds healed quickly.'

I kept silent, but I watched his face. He was talking about something that meant a lot to him, and I prayed that he wouldn't stop.

'Does the name "Vimy Ridge" mean anything to you, Jeremy?' he asked suddenly.

'It was a big battle in the First World War,' I said. That was all it meant to me. I couldn't have told you which army won the battle. I'd seen the name in print somewhere and it had stuck in my memory.

'Five-thirty pm, April 9, 1917,' the old man said quietly. He was quite obviously thinking aloud. 'We attacked then. The battle lasted six days; but not for me. In the twenty-first minute I was wounded in the chest and shoulders. I began to bleed heavily and soon I was unable to stand; but I remained conscious.'

'Just like me when Percy and I were attacked,' I thought.

'Yes,' he said slowly. 'It was, I suppose, loss of blood that made me so weak, but it might have been fear, Jeremy. If I had been able to stand, it would have been my duty as an officer to go back to the battle and lead my men forward.'

I lay as still as a mouse. I wanted him to talk. He had never talked to me like this before.

'All I knew then was that the attack on Vimy Ridge was going on without me. And, Jeremy, that thought was sweet to me. For months, I had been certain that I was going to be killed. We all expected death; and death took horrible forms in that terrible war. I could not sleep at night because the faces of dead men filled my memory. Sometimes I thought that it would be better to shoot myself than to wait for death. I'll tell you something, Jeremy, that I thought I would never tell anybody. When I lay there wounded on the battlefield, I prayed to die. I wanted to die and leave the war behind. I suppose I was a coward then, Jeremy.'

I asked, 'Why didn't you ever talk to me about this before?'

'How could I, my boy, how could I? You were only seventeen when you left home. I couldn't talk to a schoolboy about those experiences.'

'And, of course,' I said, 'I got out of military service. I didn't join the Army. You felt ashamed of me because I didn't do my duty. How could I understand the sufferings of a soldier?'

He looked at me with sad eyes. 'Don't misjudge me, Jeremy. I no longer imagine that your life must follow the same pattern as mine. I am sorry to see you lying here in hospital, but I am proud that you didn't run away when your friend was in danger. You had the courage to try to defend him. You suffered pain. You were wounded when you were helping him.'

'I'm not a hero,' I said. 'I did what I had to do.'

'And so did I, Jeremy. So did I; and thousands more like me. We were not heroes. We suffered because there was nothing else we could do. But, I tell you, my boy, those four years – from 1914 to 1918 – broke me. Since then I have had to put the pieces of my life together again. I saw men go mad in that terrible war. I saw men accused of cowardice and shot like dogs, but I knew that they were braver men than I was. My father could not understand my suffering. I tried to explain to him, but he could not imagine what a soldier's life was like.'

'And *you* never tried to explain to *me*! You talked of duty and self-discipline, but I couldn't understand why they were so important to you.'

'I don't really know why I'm telling you all this now,' he said, looking worried and unhappy.

I began to be afraid that he wanted to forget what he had

said. He was probably regretting that he had talked to me so freely. I couldn't let him slip back into his old attitudes now that we had begun to understand each other.

'You've told me about the war and about what you suffered,' I said, 'because I am lying here in a hospital bed. I haven't known pain and misery such as you have known, but I've been hurt and I've had to fight. You realize now that I'm able to look at your life with some sympathy and understanding. We've talked to each other, Dad. For the first time in our lives, we've really talked to each other.'

And we went on talking, naturally. He asked me to tell him exactly what had happened. I told him the whole story about myself and Percy and the new band. I told him about Percy's return from his tour and about the surprise that I had planned for him the night we were attacked.

While we were talking, I heard unsteady footsteps approaching my bed. It was Percy, leaning on a walking-stick, but somehow managing to smile. His head was bound up in a big white bandage which went under his chin and covered half his face as well as his head. The bandage looked like a strange kind of crown, giving him the appearance of an immense black king. He wore his hospital dressing-gown like a royal robe.

'Percy!' I said, trying to sit up.

'Don't disturb yourself,' he said. 'The nurse has allowed me ten minutes – just long enough to come over and say hello.'

I turned round and looked at the old man. He had got up from his chair and he was staring at Percy in astonishment.

'Percy,' I said, 'this is my father. Dad, this is Percy Brett.'

Percy's strong, clever black hand came forward and was met by the old man's white thin one. They shook hands across my bed.

'Glad to know you, Professor,' said Percy. The old man swallowed and spoke something polite in a low voice. Poor old boy, it was obvious that the whole thing had been a shock for him. I saw the two of them very clearly. Percy was looking more like a king than ever, his great black face shining out from those white bandages. My father was looking old, tired and rather ill. He had only his painful honesty and his terrible memories to bring to this strange meeting.

He looked from Percy to me and back again. There was something that he wanted to say, but he was having trouble in finding the right words. At last, he gave a nod in my direction and said to Percy, 'I'm sorry to see you both like this, hurt and in bandages.'

'Well, it could have been worse,' said Percy.

'Perhaps,' said the old man, 'perhaps it could, but I'm sorry to see such a sight. And so would most people be. It's a sight that makes one – makes one feel ashamed.'

I knew what he meant, and so did Percy. He was trying, in his own way, to apologize to Percy for what had been done to him. He was speaking for England and the English.

Percy raised his hands, for a second, as if to tell my father that he understood. 'Oh, well,' he said after a moment's pause, 'it happens.'

They looked straight into each other's eyes and nodded. I can't say what they were thinking. There was so much in each of them that the other could not possibly understand. But Percy's remark, 'it happens', had been exactly the right one. Both he and my father were men of peace, but they had been treated with violence. My father had been wounded by Germans because he was an Englishman. Percy had been cut and kicked by white men because he was black. 'It happens.' There was nothing more you could say.

At that moment, a nurse brought us cups of tea and a plate of bread and butter. I was glad that the conversation was interrupted. I didn't want the pressures on the old man to build up any further. He'd had enough, for one day.

When he'd drunk his tea and eaten some bread and

butter, he looked at his watch and said that he must go. He had a train to catch. Percy's ten minutes were over too. They both stood up and got ready to go.

'Well,' my father said, looking down at me. 'I shall hope for news of continued progress when your Aunt Eleanor returns from visiting you.' I noticed that he was talking in his usual stiff way. I wasn't worried. It meant nothing more than putting his hat and coat on. He was Professor Coleman again, ready to set off to catch his train. I knew that he and I were not going to lose what we'd gained that afternoon. At last, we'd really talked to each other and the old misunderstanding and distrust had gone forever.

'Don't worry,' I said, 'I'll soon be better. I'll be up and about again in a few days.'

'You must come and see us soon, Professor,' said Percy. 'We'll look quite human when we can put our clothes on.'

The old man looked at me, then at Percy, and then at me again. 'Eleanor and I will expect to see you both,' he said, 'at any time... any time you are free to pay us a visit.' He moved a few steps away, then he turned back again. 'And if Jeremy forgets,' he said, looking at Percy, 'you bring him, Mr Brett, will you?'

'Yes, I will,' said Percy.

As soon as we were out of hospital, we collected the band together and practised hard. We were good at our job and we knew it; but those early months were difficult. Our kind of music was out of fashion. It was a long time before we had any success.

I shall never forget one night when we performed in a big hall in South London. We weren't the main band. We'd been hired to play while the big rock-and-roll band was having an hour's rest. It was a terrible experience. The audience didn't want to hear us. Half-way through our performance they began a slow handclap and started shouting for the rock-and-roll 'music'. There was nothing

83

we could do. We had to clear off the stage quickly.

Percy and I paid the other members of the band and then we went to a little public house nearby. It was summertime and we sat at a table in the garden to drink our beer.

'Percy,' I said, 'our future doesn't look good.'

'The *money* doesn't look good,' he said gently, 'but nothing's happened to alter the *music*, as far as I know.'

I knew he was right. We would go on playing the music we loved. If we couldn't make a living, we'd have to get other jobs and play our jazz in our free time.

'Maybe,' Percy said, and his voice was still gentle, 'maybe that's a lesson you still have to learn. A coloured man learns the lesson early in life. He knows they can't take his music away from him. They can take everything else, but that only makes him put more into his music. You have to learn that. I grew up knowing it.'

Suddenly, I realized that I had to approach the problem in my own way. Percy had *his* approach. I had to have mine – and mine was like the old man's. You had to discover your own particular skill and then you had to work at it. You had to do the thing you were good at and give your whole life to it. That's what the old man meant by duty and self-discipline. He was a professor: I was a jazzman. We were both good at our jobs.

'Come on,' said Percy, picking up his trombone. 'There's a piano in the pub and I want to try out a new idea.'

The piano keys shone up at me as if they were smiling. There they were, my sixty-four old friends. I suppose the old man feels like that about his books. Everybody needs that feeling: the feeling that the job's worth doing.

Percy began to tap his foot. I listened for a moment, looked up at him and nodded. Then he put his horn to his lips and we started.

Exercises in Comprehension and Structure

Chapter 1 – *what*-clauses
Example: He [Jeremy's father] knew *what was best for everybody*.
Complete these sentences about the story. The facts are in Chapter 1.
1. Jazz music was what Jeremy...
2. A jazz musician was what...
3. Aunt Eleanor couldn't understand what...
4. She didn't realize what...
5. A glass of water was what...
6. What...was to lie down in the grass and rest.
7. What...was to hide it in a hedge.
8. What...was 'Where are you from?'
9. What...was working in the fields.
10. What...was that he must go back to school.

Chapter 2 – *by —ing*
Example: The club made its money *by selling* drinks and sandwiches.
Complete these sentences about the story. The facts are in Chapter 2.
1. Jeremy hid himself by...
2. By 1942 a lot of people were getting their entertainment by...
3. Jeremy earned just enough to live on by...
4. Tim attracted Jeremy's attention by...pub.
5. Jeremy could only judge an older man by...

Chapter 3 – *as if*
Example: It looks *as if* Tim had better get some cards printed.
Complete these sentences about the chapter.
1. ...as if he had grown a new set of limbs.
2. ...as if he had been introduced to a royal person.
3. ...as if he himself had taught Percy to play.
4. ...as if Tim were a child.
5. ...as if he were playing all the instruments himself.
6. Tim behaved as if...
7. Black men weren't treated as if...
8. The woman spoke to Tim as if...
9. Tim answered as if...
10. Tim's towel looked as if...

Chapter 4 – Speech verbs
There are roughly 30 verbs used in this chapter to mean the act of *speaking, using words, saying*, etc. How many can you find, and how are

they used?

(The first paragraph has *telephone, say, beg, talk, accuse*. Count each verb once only; for example, don't count *say* – or *said* etc. – in later paragraphs if you have listed it for the first. Count as one verb such expressions as *go on* – ' "You must know," I *went on*, "how Jeremy must be feeling" ' – *make enquiries*...)

Chapter 5 – Conversational English

How does Jeremy express these ideas in his story?
1. He *continued to play* softly.
2. He *suddenly* felt nervous.
3. The red-haired man wanted to *finish his work*.
4. The result would have been an unhappy conversation with *his father*.
5. His father *did not admit defeat* so readily.

Did the writer put these in on purpose? Why? Will you expect to find many similar expressions in Professor Coleman's story in Chapter 6? Why?

Chapter 6 – Reported Speech

Use this chapter to practise changing direct speech to reported speech. For example:

'Only a few hours, I'm afraid. I have to get back to work tonight.'
'Work?'...

Jeremy said he was afraid he could only stay for a few hours, as he had to go back to work that night.

The professor questioned the word 'work', and...

Chapter 7 – *that*-clauses

Answer the questions with clauses beginning '*That*'.
Example: When Eleanor heard the front door, what did she know?
Answer: That Jeremy had gone.
1. If she had run after him, what might Jeremy have thought?
2. What did the sounds in the downstairs room tell Eleanor?
3. What did Eleanor think as Alfred stood in the kitchen?
4. What was Eleanor ashamed of thinking?
5. What had Jeremy told his father about Alfred's principles?

Chapter 8 – *because*-clauses

Complete these sentences about the chapter.
1. Parisians came to the jazz clubs because...
2. Percy and Jeremy were worth hearing because...

3. They were often cold and hungry but they didn't notice it because...
4. Percy and Jeremy didn't talk together very much – except about music – because...
5. Tim was happy in Paris because...
6. Tim believed that he would be successful in America because...
7. Tim wanted Jeremy to smile because...
8. Tim trod on Jeremy's toe because...
9. Jeremy didn't tell the band about Walsheim because...
10. When Jeremy mentioned Tim, Walsheim smiled because...

Chapter 9 – —*ing*
Complete the sentences about the chapter.
Example: *Waking up was horrible* the morning after the party.
1. Giving Tim's wife his attention...
2. Supporting the children...
3. Discovering how badly Tim had behaved...
4. Writing letters...
5. Using people...
6. Going to America had been necessary...
7. Trying to be like Tim...

Chapter 10 – *How...?*
We give you the answers. Ask the questions beginning *How...*
Example: It [That period of his life] lasted ten years.
Question: *How long* did that period of Jeremy's life last?
1. He was on the radio several times.
2. He played for about forty minutes.
3. He didn't play as well as Jeremy could have played.
4. The customers never complained.
5. It was ten years since Jeremy had played like that.
6. They were in England for nine weeks.
7. They needed three more men.
8. There were six of them.

Chapter 11 – *it*
What does *it* mean in the following sentences from Chapter 11?
Example 1: *It* was painful to breathe, to eat, or to talk.
Answer: *It* = to breathe, to eat, or to talk
Example 2: 'Dear Aunt Eleanor, *it* must have been a shock for you.'
Answer: *it* = reading about the attack on Jeremy and Percy

1. I stopped smiling because *it* hurt.
2. *It* was a man, walking stiffly, and making straight for my bed.
3. 'Jeremy, my boy, *it*'s strange to see you here.'
4. 'To tell you the truth, I find *it* all very strange.'
5. *It* was going to be hard enough to find subjects for conversation.
6. '*It* was loss of blood that made me so weak.'
7. I heard unsteady footsteps approaching my bed. *It* was Percy.
8. *It* was obvious that the whole thing had been a shock for him.
9. '*It* happens.'
10. *It* meant nothing more than putting his hat and coat on.